MY
SOUL
CRIES OUT

JOYCE A. BROWN

Published by Live The Dream Publishers

South Holland, IL 60473

ISBN# 978-0-9913508-5-8
ISBN# 978-0-9913508-6-5 (eBook)

Front cover images by Navi' Robins, NorthShore Graphic Studio

Dedicated to

CHERYL M. BOX

PROLOGUE

Anna Marie heard the door slam and realized she had to face him after all. Marinating pork chops for dinner. Doing an extra load of wash. Five more minutes and the ER nurse would have been out the door and headed to the hospital. Her car keys were on the kitchen counter. Nervous energy kept her finding things that needed doing instead of listening to the morning hand-off in the Emergency Room.

Sugarman leaned on the doorbell.

Call your dad. Call Landon. Don't let him in Anna.

Ah girl, you handle hostile and belligerent assholes in the ER every weekend. Just tell him to get the hell out of your life and keep it moving.

She heard the car engine as it roared down the quiet street. He left. Confrontation avoided.

He banged on the door. Damn it! His ride drove off and left him stranded on her doorstep.

She walked swiftly to the door and yanked it open. "I told you not to come here." The smell of drugs and alcohol mixed with the

stench of prison clung to him. *God, what was I thinking?* "Get the hell away from here."

His laugh was ugly. "That's not what you said when I was sexing you up on the phone. Where the bedroom? Yo betta be ready for the rough shit. Take them scrubs off before I rip 'em off ya ass."

"Boy, you crazy?" She needed a weapon to neutralize his evil sneer.

The first blow...the first blow stunned her...

CHAPTER ONE

A *nna Marie Scott's tortured, angry, disillusioned soul floated near the ceiling of the living room, staring at the heaving man.* Rusty red foam flecks poured from Willie Earl Hoskins mouth. Blood and sweat were running like rain down his body as he straddled her prone body, pummeling her face and chest. Her beautiful dark brown round face now resembled ground beef, mangled under the punches of his brutal blood-soaked fists as he pounded five years of incarcerated shame, beating, and degradation on to her five foot, four inches, one hundred sixty-five-pound frame.

Anna's mother died when she was fifteen. Her father often commented God called the love of his life home because He needed another beautiful flower in His garden. She'd inherited her mother's face, endearing her to her widowed daddy. Now, Anna's smiling face and her sparkling lights were gone. The bones and features were shattered beyond recognition because she dared to connect with a man, heedless of the fact that he was older and incarcerated. He wasn't a killer, violent or career criminal. He was a drug dealer.

Working alongside the church's missionaries to send letters to the prisoners at Christmas at the request of the pastor's wife evolved into

a pen-pal relationship. Exchanging pictures and accepting collect phone calls escalated to riding the sixty miles to the maximum-security prison for Saturday visits with the Women's Ministry. Putting money on his book. Writing sexy letters. Talking about a nonexistent future together. Then he called to report he was getting out early for good behavior and needed her to vouch with the Parole Board that he had a stable place to stay...with her.

Willie Earl's six-foot, muscled, surly frame walked out of jail this morning. He was supposed to report to the half-way house today. His mama, who'd benefitted from the drug money days, told him straight up "don' come near me". Yet, he was driven to her home by his boys who gave him ganja, cocaine, alcohol, and pep talks on how to get a bitch in line because she wouldn't let him move in with her and her tween daughter.

Six hours later, unable to take flight, her soul was circling this serene, beautifully appointed room where she entertained family and guests. Anna was not supposed to die this soon. She still had a daughter to raise, a career, two sisters and a father. An extended family who loved and adored her.

Willie Earl hadn't overturned lamps or thrown furniture. She was the only recipient of his out-of-control rage, his bloodlust, his need for vengeance on everyone who disrespected him, treated him as less than the man he considered himself to be, ever hollered no to him. Feet encased in size twelve steel-toed combat boots stomped on her stomach and legs. Anna knew the size because she'd sent him a pair of Jordan's at Christmas. She'd felt those blows. Her kidneys. Her spleen. Her ribs cracking. Shards of bones puncturing her lungs as she choked on her blood, gurgling as she called on God to save her from this demon whose yellow and red eyes glowed. Vile words dripping from his lips. "Whore. Bitch. Have you got a man up in here? Where is he? Slut. You wouldn't answer my letters, wouldn't

come to my parole hearing, and wouldn't pick me up from jail!" She was past feeling the abuse.

Breaking it off with him was her best and worst decision. Best for repairing her relationship with the members of her extended family. Worst because as the day drew closer for his release, Willie Earl became irrational. "Gonna fuck you 'til I get the stench of this place off me! Then I'm gon' fuck you again! You betta be ready."

Who says that to a woman you met through a church prison ministry? Conversed with in a prison waiting room where contact is supervised. You hugged a couple of times. Stupid!! Telling him, she thought she loved him and wanted to see how things would go after his release. Take it slow as he made the transition to the outside.

Her father, Lee Roy Scott, begged her to take a leave from her job as an emergency room nurse. Leave town and visit her ailing grandmother down south for a few weeks until he checked him out. "You don't know him from Jack. E'ry body finds Jesus in jail, especially when Jesus is accompanied by lonely church women willin' to open their legs and ack a fool."

Lee Roy had experienced complicated relationships in his sixty-two years. He wasn't a prude or a fool. He did the best he could to raise his girls with morals and respect, talking truthfully to them about boys masquerading as men, particularly fatherless boys who ended up in prison for significant periods of their lives. Daddy warned her against sending the money and gifts. He cursed the pastor's wife for arranging the visits. He pitched a fit when her phone got shut off for accepting too many collect calls and she couldn't pay the bill.

Typically Anna did whatever her father demanded, except acknowledge that her longtime friend Landon was in love with her. She was lonely. Her baby daddy had moved on and Anna wasn't meeting men with the standards her father lived by. She'd dated

enough deadbeats, even a couple she met in the church choir. Men coveted a rent-free place to live, a sugar-momma, a drug dealer, and a woman to beat up on when the get-rich-quick schemes didn't play out in his favor.

This guy, Sugar Man was his nickname, wrote long letters sounding like he had his self together, had wrestled his demons, and sold out for Christ. She understood how he thought. At thirty-five, her life was stretching out boring, lonely, and restless. This guy might be her ticket to the good life, and she was up to the task of redeeming him.

Tiring of screaming at her unconscious pulp, the bloodlust receding from his eyes, Willie Earl dropped to the floor beside her, calling her name. "Anna Marie! Stop playin wit me, bitch! I don' wanna beat you no mo. Get up. Now!"

What the fuck is wrong with him? There's nothing left, no future for me. If I could get my soul back into my body, I'da been out of here five seconds after the first punch hit my face. I swear killing is too good for him. Before this shit is over, he'll wish he'd never heard my name.

CHAPTER TWO

*O*h, hell naw! Please, Turquoise Adele Scott!! Don't go in there! Anna tried valiantly to put out her non-existent hands to stop her daughter from unlocking the front door.

The determined twelve-year-old with freshly braided extensions was moving in time to a Rihanna song on her iPod, her earbuds firmly in place, her backpack loaded with homework, and her house key in her hand. They'd perfected her latch-key baby's routine over the years. Turquoise would enter the front door, call her granddad, fix herself a snack, turn on the computer and complete her homework. After that, she was free to text, Snapchat, tweet, do whatever kids did today until Anna finished her shift at the hospital, clocked out at 5:00 P.M. and arrived at the home to fix them a light dinner. Both mother and daughter needed to either exercise or push back from the dinner table.

"Mommy, I'm too old for a babysitter." Mommy and daughter sat down for one of their frequent family meetings with Turquoise in charge. "Besides, Masie's next door. She has a key, and I can text if I need something."

"What's the difference between you being there or here?"

"I'm growing up. Remember, when I got my period last year, you gave me this really loooong lecture about responsible behavior. You said not only was my body changing…I needed to think differently… analyze and that my decisions could have consequences." Her forever baby rocked her neck and rolled her eyes. This girl could always wrap Anna up in knots—just like her daddy. Keenan Ford could talk himself into and out of most situations, except jail.

"Besides, at Masie's, she makes me turn down the loud noise as she calls it. I don't need "day care". T put her crooked fingers up to make her point. Too much hanging around with the two aunties… Melany and Kerri.

"Alright." Anna gave in. "Let's give it a try and see. We'll re-evaluate in a couple of weeks. You might actually get lonely or scared when the furnace makes those noises."

Here's the rules. Do not open the door to anyone other than Grandpa. No guests over!! Do your homework. Do not destroy my house! Do not leave this house for any reason. Do not tell your little friends you're home alone. If I come home and find you're sneaking people into this house when I'm working…"

"STOP!!!" Turquoise launched herself into her mother's arms, hugging and kissing her until the two tumbled to the floor. "I get it."

"And there will be a list of phone numbers on the fridge door for back up."

Thursday night was teen choir rehearsal. They'd eat and leave home by 6:30 P.M. Turquoise loved hanging out with her friends and praising the Lord. The praise team was debuting a new routine on the second Sunday. Turquoise was hopeful she'd win the solo spot. For the last three months, her best friend, Afeni had upstaged her. The friends were talented, but Turquoise felt like Afeni was benefitting from some type of favoritism she didn't understand.

Right now, a solo dance was the least of Anna's worries. Please God...no!!!!!

Off-key voice blasting the Rihanna jam "Work," Turquoise's hands and body were gyrating inside the door of the living room. Turquoise would take five steps at most before discovering the bloody mass Sugar Man spat on before he grabbed her car keys and cell phone, tracked bloody prints out the front door and drove the 2010 Ford Fiesta down the street.

One second. Two seconds. Two and a half seconds. Shrieks. Screams. Fat dimpled feet in purple high-tops backin up and fleeing out the front door. Cries that could split the heavens and earth pouring out of Turquoise's mouth. Blinded by tears, running in circles, Turquoise's face was distorted by the horrific, gory scene of the woman who promised to love her forever, to protect her, to guide her to successful womanhood.

Her mama trusted the wrong man and was now swirling around her daughter's pain-wracked body. Anna was unable to console her, unable to erase the final picture of her mother imprinted on Turquoise's brain instead of the woman in pink and blue scrubs who fixed her favorite sweet potato pecan pancakes topped with warm maple syrup. A mother whose life's expiration date was unexpectedly moved up to today.

Where the hell were the nosy neighbors when you needed them? This was a middle-income neighborhood. Elders living alongside working families. Unemployed men and women mooching off family members. Anna bet they heard Sugar Man tear out of here, stripping gears and screeching tires after not driving for almost six years.

Turquoise's high-pitched shrieks finally got the attention of the next-door neighbor, Masie Cunningham, a stay-at-home mom.

Masie was still Turquoise's backup caretaker when Lee Roy was out of pocket.

The baby girl was throwing up, gagging, and screaming "Call 911... My mommy!" She dissolved in a puddle on the sidewalk, pointing to the house, whimpering like a kicked puppy. "Beaten.... Dead."

Sugar Man stole Anna's dreams of growing old in this house she'd scraped for and saved for when other women were content to live in rented apartments or their parents' spare rooms. He'd stolen her daughter's life as well. He would burn in hell. Her soul wouldn't rest until she achieved that goal.

CHAPTER THREE

Multiple police and fire department sirens rent the afternoon calm, closely followed by breaking news reporters whose lives were spent scanning police hotlines and calls for assistance. Anna chose this neighborhood because it was far removed from the usual perpetrators of violence. Neighbors poured out of their houses, walking to the edge of their property, scoping out the fire engine complete with ladder, paramedic's truck, squad cars and unmarked police sedans blocking driveways. Uniformed men and women scurried around protecting the crime scene. Reporters were taking pictures and asking officers to divulge any information about the crime scene and who was inside the house.

Police officers ignored them as they nailed stakes in the ground, wrapped yellow tape around the perimeter of the house as a black officer wearing a midnight blue suit, striped shirt, and paisley tie donned thin white gloves to inspect the blood splatter compromised by Turquoise's unknowing feet. He continually talked into a lapel microphone as the uniformed woman accompanying him scribbled notes, marking, or grabbing at items he pointed to. Crime scene investigators snapped pictures of the house and driveway and swabbed doors.

As Anna shifted, listening in on conversations, tracking the trivia and minutest details, she asked herself "Why you care 'bout a crime scene?" Cause they better get it right.

The police were attempting to determine if the attacker acted alone. There was more than enough blood, prints, and DNA waiting for them inside. There was nothing they could do for the body inside. The Medical Examiner was on her way with the wagon, body bag, and evidence-gathering tools.

"Y'all better grab that prick and get him off the streets before he kills again!" Anna screamed at the officers. With evil coursing through his veins and hopped up on drug cocktails, having felt the thrill of killing, he'll do it again. He was enjoying it. Yes, there was the rage. But there was satisfaction. A satanic rite. Unless he's stopped, he'll kill again. Next time, he'll know. He meant to harm, to immobilize, but whatever took him over was too loud, and he couldn't control the beast. He'll plan next time.

Her daddy's purple Chevy Silverado turned the corner, speeding. The screeching was nerve-wracking. Daddy needed new brakes. Lee Roy bought the purple Silverado, called it his chariot, and taught three daughters how to drive in it. He kept it in factory-like condition. Cleaning and maintaining it for the day he'd teach Turquoise to drive.

Squealing to a halt in the first available parking spot, three houses past hers, Lee Roy jumped out of the car yelling both names as though they were one. "Anna Turquoise! Anna Turquoise! Anna Turquoise!"

A middle-aged white sergeant halted his sturdy body, "Are you, Mr. Scott?"

"Yep. Who else you call?" When dealing with stress, Scott didn't tolerate dumb ass questions when the person already knew the answer.

Calm down, Daddy! Be strong for Turquoise. Your sensible daughter's Barack and Michelle's fantasy starring a convict as the leading man got her taken out. Now you must raise a fourth little girl through afterschool

activities and attitude when you're ready to enjoy fishing and pool games with your buddies at the Senior Citizens Center. Starting the next chapter with a tween girl. God help us!

My sisters, Kerri and Melany, ain't gon' be able to manage this nightmare. Guilt. Pain. Harsh words. They tried to shame me. Downloading articles from the Internet. Kerri read fiction books like "The Burning Bed." Melany poured state and national statistics about women who preferred incarcerated men down my throat like hot coffee laced with arsenic. "You're paying $3 to talk to a retard for fifteen minutes? What's goin' on in his world worth $3?"

Kerri didn't have a man, either, but that never stopped her from going out and living it up. "Anna, you fantasizing about the perfect lover. The guy only exists in your dreams because El Creepo is behind bars and not doing anything remotely worth a shit."

Both sisters told Anna she was stupid. *My butt floating around here proves I should'a been listening instead of plotting out zingers for them two broke girls. Too insecure to move on when Keenan left me after Turquoise's birth. Thinking Landon was dull because all he did was work, save money, and hang around my daddy.*

Daddy, you are stuck with a mortgage that's underwater, not enough life insurance to cover the credit card debts and a daughter too lazy to make out a will. The forced savings you made me put away and social security survivor's benefits will help. The plans for a future included me being around, healthy and working extra shifts. Once a month, she shopped for her dad at Sam's Club to make sure he had staples. Her two sisters took care of the other bills in lieu of rent. The three sisters split the tax bills. Daddy's Social Security check ought to be for him. Another reason to drop kick that asswipe through the gates of hell before either heaven or hell realizes they are missing a new soul, namely mine.

CHAPTER FOUR

Captain of Investigations, Nate Reynolds led a distraught Lee Roy Scott away from the corpse to the pine kitchen table, pulled out a seat, and pushed him into it. A six-foot-two slim hipped former wide receiver at Northwood University, Reynolds opened the refrigerator as if he lived there, pulled out two bottles of water and threw one at the older man. Lee Roy caught it reflexively. "Tell me everything about your daughter. Help us figure out who killed her." Reynolds ran the plastic bottle containing the cooling liquid across his forehead.

Anna got a glimpse of the humanity under the steel. Would he be the one to solve her murder? Why hadn't she met a replica of him when she was alive?

"I already know who kilt her." Her daddy had aged twenty years in five minutes. His skin was ashy, his hands trembled, and his voice gurgled through tears. "No good punk got released from prison this morning. He came here anyways after she told him she didn't want to see him."

"Who was he and what was his relationship with her?" Reynolds no longer presumed anything. Ask! Pry! Dig in the soft marrow until you get to the heart of the matter. "Why wouldn't she want to see him?"

Lee Roy pulled a dirty handkerchief out of his pocket, mopping tears from his face and hands. Not sure what to do with the rag, he balled it up and stuffed it back in his pocket. "Where do I start?"

"Wherever you feel like it." Reynolds' prying eyes were surprisingly kind. He didn't fidget. He sat there, waiting as her father collected his thoughts. Reynolds heard versions of this story numerous times over the years. He was good at this part of the job.

"My Anna was a good girl, wanting to act like … 1 don't know … like dem people in books are real." Scott looked like he was sucking on lemons. "When the right man comes along, he gonna be a prince and whatever happened before will be ancient history. Life ain't like books. Men are dogs."

Reynolds sniggered. Because he'd been accused of having doggish ways, he knew what Scott was alluding to.

"What I meant is men like the chase. I raise huntin' dogs; I know how they act. Once dem dogs get the bone, the prize, the whatever, they on the hunt again. It takes a strong woman to make a man understand she ain't gonna put up with doggish behavior. My wife, God rest her soul, died too soon. I did a good job, except for Anna. She smart, well-educated, got a respectful baby girl, but she wants a man. A man to complete her, make her feel whole. I tried to tell her only a whole woman can find a whole man. She never got what I meant."

Reynolds nodded. He'd spent enough time in vice to understand how a lot of women ended up on the streets trying to please a man

or being turned out to support some bum's drug habit. He didn't miss those days.

"We brought the girls up in the church. Because of a prison ministry set by the preacher's wife, Anna goes on a field trip to the Ionia State Prison and meets Willie Earl Hoskins. He was serving a six-year sentence for drugs with intent to distribute. He calls himself Sugar Man. He was released early this morning after midnight." Scott broke down again.

"When was the last time you talked to your daughter?"

The older mam swiped at his eyes and blew his nose. "Last night. I begged her to take a vacation, leave town." Lee Roy had talked until as he muttered 'he was purple in the face,' begging, and bargaining with her.

Judging her like a stupid person who'd let a man abuse her. As it happened, Anna was no match for Sugar Man's sneak attack. She was on the floor with one punch to the stomach less than five minutes after he entered the house.

"Why did you want her to leave?" Reynolds pushed for more details. The most irrelevant information could lead to the arrest of this perp and peace for the family.

"He was nuts, a head case, and she couldn't see it. Too trusting. Fancied herself in love until he started talkin' like somebody out of Looney Tunes." Scott wiped at his face with a towel on the table.

"Give me an example." Reynolds pinched his nose with two fingers, spoke Willie Earl's name and the prison he'd been released from into his lapel, then barked, "Get me a status update on his release and the name of his parole officer."

Lee Roy's eyes stared as though he could look through the wall into the room where the remains lay. His youngest daughter didn't

want to live in his old Washington Heights neighborhood where people and activities were changing for the worse. Now her bodily fluids were oozing into the cream colored wool carpet he'd purchased for Anna when she bought this house.

Daddy, you were spot on. You warned me that the East, West, South or North side of town wouldn't matter. You drilled into me there are good people along with the criminal element in the neighborhood where I was raised. Moving across town meant I got an updated floor plan, higher taxes, and neighbors who don't give a damn about me.

"Hoskins had it in his head to move in here with her and Turquoise." Lee Roy scrubbed his hands down his face, turned his back to Reynolds until he could recover from the shudders wracking his body. "Over my dead body was she letting him move in here with a twelve-year-old girl and he been locked up for most parts of six years. She didn't know him. Any fool can con you when it means three meals and a bed with a willing woman. Step up from prison. He wasn't going straight. I don't give a damn what the preacher's wife insisted. She ain't no authority on jailbirds. First Lady got herself a brother in prison, and this so-called interest is so she can help him out. Niggas get on my nerve pretending. It was nothing but a con and now my baby girl is dead."

How come her know-it-all-self didn't have any inkling the ministry was a con? She needed to get her head out of the books and into the real world. A nurse dealing with victims of gun violence, drug abuse, domestic battery, yet Anna kept a world vision even her colleagues questioned. Work, church, taking care of her daughter, visiting with family. Never a party girl, only an occasional wine drinker with her sisters.

Captain Reynolds lifted his eyebrows a couple of inches, lines furrowing his forehead, and shook his head. "Mr. Scott, we see a

lot of this. Lonely women entrapped by cons who see these women as a meal ticket or a patsy."

Reynolds pushed tissues toward my daddy who was unaware of tears falling on his hands and dripping onto my floor which I'd mopped last night, praying Sugar Man would go to his family.

"We have to find him. He's a ticking time bomb. If he did this to your daughter, who knows what he'll do next?" Reynolds stood up, looked at his watch, and shook Lee Roy's damp hand. "The county medical examiner is on her way to remove your daughter's body. You've been very helpful. I've got to follow-up on what you gave me. " As an afterthought he turned around, "Mr. Scott, I'm sorry for you loss. We'll find him."

Reduced to a soul without a body and angry at her gullibility, Anna would find Sugar Man and stop him. Her murder wouldn't go unsolved like so many others in this small town.

CHAPTER FIVE

*A*fter the medical examiner determined the time of death by checking the pooled fluids and removing the body from the house, Anna's soul gained energy. Her first stop was Liberty International Nondenominational Church with six hundred members, most of them single women and children. Maybe she could figure out the answers here. Retrace her steps. Reflect on the new information she'd gained and apply the instructions she'd received differently...be prayerful and helpful without crossing any lines.

She hovered on the ceiling light fixture in the First Lady's office. Look at the woman with her make-up streaked and that crooked weave on her head. With new insights, Anna saw signs of the manipulative sister under the makeup and expensive clothing. Why did the first lady organize and operate the Prison Ministry? Wasn't that something the men should be doing? Women could still help with supplies and prayers.

"Can you help a sister out?" First Lady asked Delphina Holmes, another woman following in Anna's relationship-challenged footsteps. Like Anna, Delphina was too eager to please the spiritual mother of the church. Had Anna only heard what she wanted to hear? No discernment. No talking to her sisters who thought she'd lost her mind.

"We need to send Lenten cards to approximately two hundred inmates." First Lady Lenore Watson smiled. "It will only take an hour." The same syrupy story she'd used on Anna and other women when she needed someone to do the actual work of ministry. The religious leader would lay out everything after the administrative assistant developed and printed the materials. Some unsuspecting souls always offered to help.

Try hand addressing two hundred envelopes, filling them, and sticking on stamps. Think, girl. She's roped you into four hours of work. And now comes her patented lie.

"The others should be along soon; more hands will make the work go quicker."

Too bad Anna couldn't slap the taste out of First Lady's mouth. Looking at Lenore Watson, having heard her daddy say the woman's brother was also locked up at Ionia. Anna screamed at the two-facedness of the woman. First Lady spoke of doing God's work. Was this all a cover to help her brother? Was Anna collateral damage?

Delphina beamed. "Sister Watson, I'm glad you asked me to help out. We're so proud of the commendation you're receiving from the governor tomorrow for ten years of prison ministry."

"I always say favor ain't fair, but it sure looks fabulous." First Lady preened like a flamingo, raking her long red nails across the front of her peacock blue suit. Regardless of the day or the task, Sista Gurl was decked out in a designer suit, high heels, flashy jewelry, and full makeup. But when prison visitation day arrived, Sister Watson always had a last-minute conflict or emergency. She left the visit management to whoever was her major suck-up of the moment.

"Are you going to touch on the personal relationships that develop between the women and the inmates in your acceptance speech?" Delphina asked. Moving beyond mission to personal relationships or fraternizing with inmates was one of the first lady's pet peeves. They were there to do God's work. If Anna was being honest, the woman admonished them to remember why they were there before every trip to the prison. Prisoners confused caring spirits with real life relationships because they were lonely or deprived of real family interactions. She spoke endlessly to the women about how to wait on God to send them a decent man, to stop fornicating, and to let God direct them.

Hell, no! I don't condone such behavior." Sister Watson's dreadful weave snapped up, her eyes flashing. First Lady snarled. "We're ministering for healing and restoration, not telling folks to get their freak on." She stared Delphina down until the younger woman looked away.

"Sorry, First Lady. I didn't mean to upset you!" Delphina gazed up at the light fixture, and her eyes almost bugged out.

Could Delphina see Anna perched up there wanting to wrench the light fixture from the ceiling and plunge it on to the high-priced desk the single women's ministry purchased for First Lady at Christmas? Better yet, cut it down and throw it on First Lady. She might not promote intimate relationships, but Anna met this man because she was listening to this woman's half-truths.

First Lady composed herself and spoke in intimate sharing tones. "I'm sorry I was so sharp with you. Those pilgrimages are a part of our mission to follow Christ's teachings. You have no idea how offended and distraught I am that Anna is even thinking about a relationship with that man outside of the prison walls! Pastor and I met with Brother Scott last week, and he's threatening to leave the

church, blaming us for Anna's bad decisions." First Lady reached across the table to pat Delphina's shaking hand. "Am I upsetting you with my blunt speech, Sister Delphina?"

A trembling Delphina averted her eyes, looking up at the pulsing red light again, shook her head and refocused on First Lady spewing venom.

"We learned Anna's been carrying on a boyfriend-girlfriend relationship with Willie Earl Hoskins for two years. He's getting out of prison soon, bypassing his home and support system to come to live with her." First Lady's right hand fretted with the diamond tennis bracelet on her left arm. "What kind of example is she setting for her darling Turquoise?"

"Have you spoken to her?" Delphina's attention was distracted from her flowing script writing the men's name, prison identification number and address on each envelope while savoring the news she was privy to. Miss Prissy Anna Marie Scott was going to shack up with a man who'd spent years in jail. Against her will, Delphina was pulled back to the blinking light above them.

Sister Watson's voice was strident as she continued her tirade. "Anna rolled her eyes and her neck, pointed her trigger finger in my face and snapped at me. I've never seen that uncontrollable side of her before. It's not appropriate for a woman with a pre-teen daughter to be focusing on her carnal desires." First Lady clenched the pen in her hand as though it was Anna's neck. "Foolishness grieves my spirit. I begged her to come back here for a prayer session with the mothers of the church after she calms down. Hopefully, she'll be here tonight with Turquoise, and we can get her to see reason."

First Lady must not have heard the news yet. The police have an APB out for Willie Earl Hoskins but are keeping the murder under wraps for fear of alarming the public. Anna blew out an exasperated breath, and

the lights blinked. Oh, my God! She did it again, and the lights went out for a minute.

Delphina squirmed in her seat like she was ready to pee in her pants.

"What is wrong with the ceiling lights?" First Lady finally picked up her phone and pushed a button. "Let me call maintenance to check them out."

The room's lights flashed on and off. Both women looked as if God were issuing a warning against gossip and slander.

First Lady screamed at whoever answered, "Get the maintenance man over here right now. The lights in my office are flickering and cutting off and on."

Gone was the bravado. Better recognize God don't like ugly and First Lady is sitting here talking about a murder victim even if she doesn't know it yet.

First Lady kept cutting her eyes at the blinking ceiling fixture, drumming her shaky fingers on her desk. "I wonder what foolishness Anna is gonna say tonight. I told her to cut off this relationship. It's a trick of the devil, a dark spirit she entertained. She didn't know him except through letters and a few visits where there were fifty other people in the room. There are decent, God-fearing men already in the church she should set her sights on."

Delphina asked, "Do you feel the same way about the men who come here from the half-way house to assist Mrs. Marble in the soup kitchen? Mrs. Marble goes to the half-way house and hand-picks the men she wants. She checks them out of the center on Saturday morning and drives them back there when the soup kitchen is cleaned up after dinner." Delphina was trying to turn the conversation away from Anna to safer topics.

First Lady shook her head. "Mrs. Marble does her own thing. She's an elder who has a camaraderie with these men. They respect her counsel, and she's no pushover."

"But the young women around here are looking at them. What are you going to say to them?"

Yeah, First Lady. Same kind of men who served time in prison. Living in a half-way house. Good enough to volunteer in your soup kitchen, but not good enough to socialize with the young single women in the church.

The first lady cocked her head.

Wanting to remain on the right side of the first lady, Delphina spoke soothingly. "Mrs. Marble knows the program director personally. He went to high school with one of her daughters."

"The Director checked out the men before letting them hang out with a seventy-three-year-old woman." First Lady nodded approvingly. "Befriending these men who've served time behind bars does not require crossing the line into a personal relationship. How can I get these lonely women to see Christ as head of their lives, to be content with Him until He sends a Boaz to redeem them?"

First Lady had continually put widowed and single men in Anna's path, and she made a detour around them for her crush. Too late now. Anna limited herself to a broken man who was in her sightline instead of waiting for God to send her a man who would be the provider and mate she desired.

Hovering atop the light fixture gave her the missing perspective that landed her here, dead but unable to rest in peace. Too late! Anna slipped on household bills to hold Sugar Man down and asked the church's benevolence committee for help. They turned her down. Anna would never ask those hypocrites for a penny again. Anna stopped confiding in First Lady when the older woman asked why Anna was shortchanging her household to put money on Hoskins' book.

Livid at First Lady, Anna rejected Sister Watson's words, "The church is there to give alms to the poor and visit those in prisons. The prison ministry is not a playground to meet men, to find a boo or a potential life mate. It's stretching the definition and purpose of the benevolence fund to give money to a working woman who's making unwise choices."

Several of the chandelier's gold and silver bangles fell when Anna huffed on it. She might not have a voice or a body, but she had power.

Delphina jumped up, spilling cards and lists as she ran toward the door.

"Delphina, what has you so spooked? It's a mechanical problem. The maintenance men will it get fixed."

Delphina's back was pressed against the door, her legs, shaking. "My granny used to talk about spirits ... feels like chills and pain in this room ... eerie like a soul's locked out of heaven. Sumthin' ain't right."

"What's not right is testing God's patience with foolishness. Pray for Anna to be delivered before it's too late." First Lady walked over to a shelf of materials she'd purchased after her chat with Anna. Statistics on relationships between women and men behind bars. Articles urging women to protect themselves from predators. The addresses of domestic violence shelters and counseling programs in the area where women could turn for counseling and other assistance.

"In this church, we don't believe in that old mess about spirits. Let it go." Sister Watson looked directly at Delphina. "I love Anna; I even placed her name in my Bible asking God to open her eyes, increase her natural and supernatural eyesight."

CHAPTER SIX

"What the fuck do you want me to do?" Reynolds scowled at the two women investigators who'd been left at the Scott residence to finish processing the crime scene. Lt. Sylvia Goldberg and Sgt. Simmons were in his office wasting his time. Anybody passing by the partially open door could see and hear him berating the two female officers. "You want me to redirect resources to finding this douche bag. We got gangs tearing up the city, shooting random folks. A sniper's been on the loose for months, and three little children were stuffed in a freezer for no damn reason."

"Hoskins will kill again. The signs are there." Lieutenant Sylvia Goldberg was head of the Police Department's Domestic Violence Task Force. While walking alongside Reynolds at the crime scene, she was evaluating it differently than he did as the basis for finding this murderer. The escalating violence. At times, Goldberg envisioned, the perp knelt over Anna, battering her at close range after she was incapacitated. Reynolds would laugh at her if she mentioned to him how the brutality and negative energy were still bouncing around the living room and throughout the house. He'd call her superstitious and block her chances of getting out of the BCPD.

These ferociously inhumane battery cases were increasing. The response from Goldberg's superiors was to blame the victim. They pointed out the number of calls from women claiming abuse yet refusing to press charges. In cases where the officers were forced to file charges or face disciplinary action, the woman declined to testify. If the sicko bastard killed the victim, women's groups went to the newspaper, appeared on television, and wrote op-eds about ineffective police protection for females. Things weren't much better for female officers. They were the butt of office jokes, given demeaning jobs and ridiculed for acting like men when they should be home instead of taking jobs meant for men.

Anna strained to push her will between the two combatants. Wait, put a pin in it my brotha and my sista. My murder is not domestic violence/ domestic battery, whatever the word is for men who take extreme pleasure in beatin' up helpless and hapless women. We were never close to being in bed together. Anna lighted on Reynold's coffee cup handle and flipped the scalding hot coffee onto his suit pants and jacket.

Reynolds pushed back, and his ergonomic chair's casters prevented him from toppling over. He curled his lip and brushed off the coffee stains from his pants. "I'm sick to death of these domestic abuse cases!" He stood, pulled off his jacket and threw it across the room where it landed on a battered chair.

He was grouchy, Goldberg mused. Reynolds never lets a day go by without a joke about men insisting on their rights in the workplace and at home. He'd come up through the ranks, worked vice and prostitution, and openly demeaned women. She'd love to follow him home. Instead, she kept careful notes of offenses he committed against women both in the office and in the line of duty. He'd never be chief which was his principal goal. After all the crap he'd tried to pull against her and equally qualified women, she would emerge as the woman who took him down.

Goldberg rubbed her hands over her face and mouth open as she stared at the coffee staining the floor underneath his chair. Reynolds drank gallons of coffee daily, and she'd never seen him spill a drop. What was she missing? This case was in its infancy, and the sniping was already at the boiling temperature. Her Spidey senses were on high alert and a ripple ran down her spine.

"Shit!" Reynolds spoke through gritted teeth. "When we catch this son-of-a-psycho the most we can hold him on is the parole violation until the medical examiner completes the forensic autopsy. Putting out extra manpower is not going to happen. This case is not a priority." He gave them the side-eye. "Don't you have real cases to work on? Lieutenant and Sergeant, just do your damn jobs. This is not your usual domestic violence case."

Goldberg and Sergeant Jamie Simmons unsuccessfully hid their angry eyes, raging silently at the unfair distribution of resources. Goldberg slammed the door as they walked out and turned toward their tiny office, ignoring colleagues who wanted the 411 on the murder case. Their office was designed for one person, usually a captain, but because of the lack of respect for their work, it was headquarters for The Domestic Violence Task Force. They'd crammed another scarred desk and bookcase in the room. Overflowing evidence boxes were stacked below the one small window and strewn papers added to the chaotic working conditions. Visitors stood because there was no room for visitors' chairs.

Simmons muttered under her breath. "If it were a member of his family, his smug ass would be all over this. Word around here is he's been known to throw a fist upside his woman's head in the heat of the moment."

"Sergeant, shut up! We got enough going on without getting charges for malicious gossip from our supervisor." Goldberg's temples

pumped blood, and icy tendrils swirled through her brain. She needed to ignore the interference. "There's enough blood, hair, and other DNA mixed with hers. A rookie at the academy knows Hoskins can be charged without waiting for the autopsy."

"What do we do?" Simmons was modeling her career after her savvy street mentor, including planning to take over The Domestic Violence Task Force when Goldberg left for someplace where her talents were appreciated. It was no secret that the department wanted her gone. She made the men look inept and had found enough corruption in the department to be permanently labeled both a bad-ass and a pain in the ass. Having family members in the department did not help either. Her father retired as Chief. Her brothers were well respected in the department. They were constantly ribbed about their younger sister, but the comments stopped short of disrespect.

Goldberg set her sights on getting hired at the Grand Rapids Police Department. At the metropolitan police department, she'd be able to use and expand the skills she'd gained in her forensic science master's program and her recent internship at Quantico. The patronage of family members hadn't helped her advance here. Small town policing was about who you knew and whether you played by the good-old-boys' rules. As the youngest and only girl in the family, her brothers taught her self-defense, martial arts, and how to read men. It wasn't enough to have the martial arts skills. She had to think like them, talk like them, and back up any shit she laid out there.

Goldberg's run-ins with the brass when speaking out about domestic violence resulted in negative reviews and being overlooked for promotion. The underground at BCPD swore Reynolds was a dirty cop and she'd better watch her back. Goldberg's antenna confirmed her superiors were waiting for one misstep and she'd be fired. Disgraced. Blackballed.

Last month, she'd been disciplined for intervening when Jerald Dowling, a business executive and local civic leader refused to allow emergency medical treatment for his severely beaten wife. The battered woman's previous beating landed her in the local Emergency Room. It took a sizeable personal donation from Gerald Dowling and another one from the family-owned company to create a new pediatric wing to cover up that debacle. The woman was eventually transported to a Lansing hospital where her broken ribs were tended to.

Goldberg cleared her mind and snapped back to her colleague. "What we always do. Launch our own investigation." Goldberg was fascinated by the picture of Anna Scott she'd lifted from her house. Eyes dancing, mouth turned up in a big smile, she was boogying with her sisters and her daughter. The sheer exuberance of living was there in the tilt of her head and the sway of her hips in skinny jeans and ankle-strapped high heels.

Goldberg fidgeted and put down the picture. She was distressed by an incessant buzz at the base of her skull, knowing someone was trying to infiltrate the back door to her mind. If she could just find a method of shutting down, the voice would go away. But work was not a place to shut down. She'd just have to deal with whatever happened.

"Count me in. I'm riding with you, Thelma and Louise."

CHAPTER SEVEN

A nna didn't dare go near her family's Ann Avenue home yet. Witnessing their devastation, destroyed by her actions, this was not a scene she could deal with right now. Would Kerri or Melany assist her daddy in explaining to Turquoise who killed her mommy and why? Their sorrow mixed with anger at Anna's death would morph into fury at First Lady for indirectly facilitating the relationship. Her sisters would demand answers from the police and stir up trouble within the church.

Which of her father's six brothers' would make the funeral arrangements when her body was released? Could they even have a funeral with the damage to her face and upper body? No way could her face be shown in public unless they wanted Turquoise to end up in an asylum. Thankfully, her baby girl only glimpsed the bloody scene before high-tailing it out of there.

Anna's ride-or-die girlfriends were shattered. As the news filtered out, they'd showed up in mass, taking over her daddy's house. Tonight, and for days afterward, the drinks would flow. Whiskey shots for Anna. Jokes. Stories. The only way to face death was with grim humor, masking the pain, unwilling to ask or answer the questions

spinning around the house she'd grown up in, where she'd conceived and bore Turquoise.

Nobody with sense would be going anywhere near her house. Not only was yellow tape strung around the place, but blood splatters were in the driveway. Two plain-clothes cops sat in an unmarked sedan watching to see if Sugar Man returned to the scene of his crime. If the bitch had any sense, he'd head west and keep going. But with little gas in the car, he wouldn't get far unless he left jail with money. He'd run out of her house without stealing hers.

Right about now, the town's gossips, jealous bitches, and thugs had twenty different versions of what had happened in her home. The lies and guesswork would consume social media. Members of her distant family would likely learn her fate on Snapchat or Twitter. Disbelieving sane, sensible, church-going Anna was carrying on a secret relationship with an inmate at Ionia Prison. Her aunts might know Jesus, but they were street enough to beat folks down. Best not say anything publicly against Anna.

Anna perched on Goldberg's keyboard screen, fascinated by the speed and intensity of the woman's mind. The cop's layers of defenses were tough, yet Anna kept pushing, hoping to find an in. Until today, Anna only knew Lieutenant Goldberg by reputation. Sylvia Goldberg's reputation for taking down men who beat women made her the darling of local women's groups. Goldberg spoke to victims about their rights. She trained social service providers to collect reliable witness statements. She received commendations and spoke at community rallies to support the victims of domestic violence.

Goldberg channeled her work-related anger into resolving the case while Reynolds sat on his ass doing nothing other than the required minimum before he'd be forced to talk to the press. His energy was focused on his next promotion. He'd graduated with a

master's degree in Criminology and Police Science two years ago. As the highest-ranking African American in the BCPD, the brass showcased him when high profile cases within the African American community demanded an immediate response instead of their usual lack of resources or empathy.

"Jamie, get me everything available on the perp." Goldberg's eyes bore into the screen, taking note of every detail compiled from the various perspectives on the scene earlier. This screen contained most of the elements linked to finding this perp and taking him down hard. What had cops done before technology allowed them to speak the facts, the suspicions, and the evidence into a lapel microphone and spit out the minutiae of a thirty-five-year-old woman's death?

"Reynolds has his prior drug-related conviction and trial information." Jamie hunched forward, scribbling on the yellow legal pad.

There was a leader and a follower in this duo. Must make for long days. Until Anna could devise a better plan, she needed to digest what they knew. Ole boy was not getting away with killin' her after she befriended him, gave him her time and money. He'd caused her daughter to become an orphan.

"Is there only one copy of the file?" Goldberg threw up her hands in disgust. "You bowl with those folks down in IT. Five minutes and the file better be on my screen."

Jamie picked up the office phone on her desk, her right pointer finger poised over the buttons debating who to call.

Because she multitasked as a way of life, Goldberg demanded her assistant to do the same. Details were missing from Goldberg's comprehensive file. "Jamie, please get me whatever info you can dig up on her car. Check DMV, find out where she bought it."

Jamie rolled her eyes and nodded, finally pushing in the numbers for IT. While waiting for someone to pick up, she tapped her personal phone to get info on the missing car.

When Jamie finished her tasks, Goldberg ticked off the plan of action. "We have two phone calls on the recorder. Both were from her employer. The first about five minutes after she's due to report in. The second about an hour later. The perp's in the wind when the second call comes in. We get a bead on the car; we're closer to finding him or figuring out where he's headed. Hoskins has minimal money, and he needs a change of clothes. He's covered in blood splatter. Hoskins can only go to a couple of places without either being turned away or folks calling 911. Even in the hood, you don't want to get crossed up in the aftermath of bludgeoning a woman to death. Accessory after the fact. Aiding and abetting. Felony murder. If we catch a break, we get him before Reynolds figures out we're not working on the domestic violence cases he assigned us."

Damn straight. Finally, some action. Anna wished she could hug Goldberg. Instead, she bounced from the keyboard to the lieutenant's shoulder. We are linked until this is over.

Goldberg shuddered. Was it Babs trying to reach out to her? The lieutenant anticipated the woman might eventually trust her enough to listen to the multiple reasons why she needed to extricate herself from Gerald before he killed her. The man was raging. You didn't need a degree in victimology to see it. Every time some community organization complimented Barbara, or she was recognized for her good deeds, he brutalized her.

CHAPTER EIGHT

"Goldberg, three women were putting money on his books. Mama. Ex-girlfriend. Anna." Simmons squinted as she read the information she'd obtained from IT. She rarely wore her glasses at work. They didn't fit her image of a hard-hitting cop. Her contact lenses were scratched, so she leaned over her screen, squinting at the information. "Damn, he must have been a balla with money."

Goldberg leaned back in her chair and put her feet up on the desk, crossing them at the ankles, exposing her small revolver. She swiped at her shoulder, shrugging off the slight tension. "Something's not adding up. With three women bankrolling you, why not go to live with the one who wants you the most."

"And plot your revenge on the guys who ratted you out." Simmons ran her pointer up and down the lines of money banked and expenditures. "For eighteen months, Anna sent between fifty dollars and one hundred dollars on the first of the month, more than the other two women combined. Anna stopped sending money three months ago. Willie Earl's mother sent ten or twenty dollars every

39

couple of weeks. The ex-girlfriend sent about the same. The other two women continued putting money on the books right up to last week."

"Why murder your primary ex-sponsor within six hours of leaving prison?"

Anna could have kicked her own stupid butt. Every dollar she faithfully posted on his books could have purchased added life insurance for Turquoise. Her father was too old to pick up a third job. His military benefits and two part-time jobs covered his needs but were not enough for Turquoise's expenses.

"Anna's money stopped around the time Hoskins met with the parole board." Goldberg double checked her timeline. "Hit up Samson and ask him what the deal was." Samson was one of the senior guards assigned to the unit where Hoskins was housed. He ran a tight, although crooked group where discipline was swift and lethal.

"Samson would rather talk to you." Her office mate batted her baby blue eyes at Goldberg and smirked, making sure she was out of the way of flying objects. Her partner was not known for playing nice. While labeled a hard-ass, Goldberg's long legs and trim body were admired by her colleagues. Because they only saw her in uniform, they men speculated about what lay beneath the blues. They knew she worked out regularly because she kicked their asses regularly in drills. Her brothers' wives stopped playing matchmaker because she ran the poor guys off with her police stories and lack of feminine wiles.

"Harrumph! Not happening. Samson is either on the take or running the illicit drug and sex rings. Not my idea of a person I want to build a relationship with." Disillusioned by the toll the stress of dealing with rapists, murders, mentally ill, and violent prisoners were taking on too many of her fellow corrections and law enforcement

officers, Goldberg's solemn oath was not to get intimately involved with her comrades. That left her with few men to choose from. Her job was her life.

The lieutenant dropped her feet to the floor, stood up and ran a hand across the back of her neck, underneath her thick dark hair. She couldn't dispel the edginess in the room. The last time she'd felt this pressure, it was her grandmother stalking her from the grave until Sylvia reconciled with her mother over choosing police work instead of marrying a wealthy Jewish boy and having three or four babies.

Simmons placed the call, putting the prison guard on speakerphone. Goldberg shot the younger woman the third finger salute as Samson yelled, "Hey, Sweet Cheeks. Been waiting for yo' call since we got the news about the mofo."

"What do you know?" Ignoring his suggestive behavior was better than any other method Goldberg tried.

The corrupt guard growled, playing along. "When Sugar Man, I don't know where he got the name, showed up here, he was sniveling and crying like a bitch. He might have had skills and rep in a small-town pond. His bulk was a deterrent to those wannabe thugs and low-life drug dealers. He came here with junkyard dogs who bench press three hundred fifty pounds and up, and call gang-fights to stay in practice. The Detroit n-words, Native Americans from the Upper Peninsula, white supremacists, and Hispanics either have the scars or claim they busted numerous heads in fights."

Anna's angry pulsations were getting bigger and darker with every new piece of information. She was the only one believing in this man. She hovered around Goldberg, picking up on her vibrations. Why wouldn't Goldberg acknowledge the connection between them?

"Cons scared the piss out of him." Goldberg and Simmons knew the drill about prison indoctrination. Goldberg was too distracted to catch more than a hint of the supernatural forces flitting around her. In addition to bantering with Samson, her phone kept pinging. She ignored the calls.

"If you ain't affiliated in here, you in trouble. Sugar Man was a target from the moment he stepped off the bus shackled to the guys in front and back of him. With his sniveling, he got tripped. He ended up on suicide watch after being gang-raped and beat down."

Simmons needled Samson. "Aren't your people supposed to protect the new guys, guide 'em through the process of socialization?"

"Slow learners get through for a fee or services. You've been up here to interrogate the vermin we get." Samson chortled.

Goldberg hated the prison block walls, the locks closing behind staff as they moved from one pod with its open space ringed with two-person cells to another. Even with surveillance cameras, she was sweating like a pig on a dry summer day and couldn't wait to get back to Battle Creek for a shower and to delouse in case she encountered the visible four-footed vermin.

Samson's voice dropped, tense and choppy. "The guards worry about shivs to the ribs, getting their share of the drugs, and making it to retirement. We not babysittin' preschoolers."

Goldberg heard officers yelling from the bullpen. She didn't have much time before Reynolds or one of the other captains came screaming for her. "Give me anything I can use to catch this som'bitch."

Samson smacked his lips, a loud sound for her benefit. "While Sugar Man was in solitary, one of the guards took pity on him and offered him protection for a fee. The reasonable amount grew over time. If he was short of money, he paid in other ways. Sugar Man figured out how to smooth talk lonely women. Most of the money on his book paid for security. None of these women would've given him the time of day if they met him on the street. Ugly ways, petulant, a wannabe bully. Whenever a woman figured out the con, he moved on to the next one."

Anna and Goldberg hit the same frequency at the same time. The temperature dropped, and lightning shot through Goldberg. Goldberg's body shook, and she began prowling around the cluttered room attempting to dislodge a tenacious Anna Scott.

"Things got tense around here recently when one of his women stopped putting money out there. His last few months weren't easy for him." Samson cursed. "Is that who he kilt?"

"Yep," Goldberg confirmed. "Any advice for us?"

"Check out the other woman. Then his mama. I'm not sure if the addresses on file are correct. The money comes through a wire transfer service." Samson informed her. "I can't wait to see him after you get through with him. He'll be caught off guard by a couple of women officers. He'll think he can do to you what he did to that defenseless woman." Samson's belly laughs rumbled through the confined space. "Shall we keep his bunk waiting for him?"

Goldberg flexed her fists. No way would Sugar Man get the jump on her like a defenseless Anna. Growing up in a family of cops, she'd learned how to brawl from the best as her uncles, brothers, and father tried to prevent her from entering the academy fresh out of college with a degree in psychology and criminal justice. She worked out regularly with the guys, was a black belt in mixed martial arts and kept a cool head.

"Hoskins is headed back to Ionia or the graveyard. I don't particularly care which one it is." Goldberg threw several punches

upside the head of an invisible Hoskins. "Murder with special circumstances."

"It doesn't get any worse than this." Samson was quiet for a minute. "Hoskins' old roommate will be glad to have him back."

"I owe you, Samson."

CHAPTER NINE

"Simmons, follow-up with the medical examiner and the forensic pathologist." Once she'd entered the information dump from Samson, Goldberg read aloud the list of names and information they needed to move on in this case. Her voice cracked as she rattled off the list to the sergeant. Her instincts demanded she act quickly to contain this guy. "Check on the APB. How hard is it to spot a 2010 Ford Fiesta? There aren't that many routes headed out of town. Are we the only ones working this murder investigation? Has anyone contacted the ex or his family members?"

Goldberg had given up on attempts to change Reynolds' views about domestic violence. BCPD's over-sexualized rape-culture didn't prioritize catching perps who violated women. After ten years on the force, her skin hardened but not her resolve. Anna deserved an impartial investigation and resolution. No man had the right to abuse, terrorize, or kill a woman because she refused him money, sex, or a place to live.

Goldberg strode back and forth, attempting to dislodge a chattering Anna Scott. She didn't have time for the woman. She had to maintain her focus on catching the murderer. "We're less

than crud underneath Reynolds' fingernails. Hack into the captain's files to see if he's got anything he's not sharing. "

Domestic violence was pitted against gang violence when the department was forced to shell out limited resources. The Gang Squad deserved its funding, but puh-leeze. In this town of fifty thousand people, the cops knew every gang banger. The Gang Squad could clean them out in a month if they wanted to give up their cushy jobs of hobnobbing with "gang leaders," and "community leaders", speaking at rallies instead of arresting thugs.

Hallelujah! It's about time you got righteous about me.

Goldberg's eyes widened. The hair on her arms and neck stood up along with raised bumps. She looked at Simmons, who was on the phone, talking to IT and jotting down notes. "Simmons, did you say something?" Goldberg interrupted her subordinate.

With a negative shake of her head, Simmons continued jotting down notes. Both officers knew Goldberg demanded correct, thorough information. Goldberg used every case to uplift the cause of women. For Simmons. it was a job, not a calling. Jamie Simmons was subjected to verbal and nonverbal abuse on too many occasions when she made mistakes.

It's about time you recognized I'm in the mix, Lieutenant Goldberg.

Goldberg's hands slapped her cheeks. "We've been working non-stop since we hit the crime scene. I don't need interference right now."

Simmons gave her a perplexed look as she hung up the phone and reached for a can of Coke and her ever-present peanuts. "Goldberg, you returned from Quantico three days ago. You were in a great head space. You can't be worried yet."

Goldberg walked to the small window which opened out on the police department's parking lot, leaned her head on the cold

glass and pushed against the cobwebs in her brain. The new police building was being constructed there, and she hoped to be gone before it was finished.

Lt. Goldberg, it's me. Anna Marie Scott. Talk to me. Stop acting like you don't hear me.

"Anna?" Goldberg's head ached. Her anger over Reynolds' cavalier treatment of this case was clouding her judgment. Damn ghosts. Barbara Dowling and Anna Marie Scott. Voices talking in her head. She would be institutionalized if anyone knew she had what they called second sight. The first time it happened was when Goldberg's mother's best friend descended into madness and accessed Goldberg's back door. When Sylvia told her mother about the voices, Mom cackled, "Shut up Sylvie. My friend is just odd." Four years later, the friend was a long-term resident at Kalamazoo's Psychiatric Hospital.

You don't believe it's me. Check this out.

The desk radio, still in the off position, blasted Rhianna's "*Rude Boy*." Battle Creek did not have a black radio station.

Damn. Not now. Not again. Goldberg needed a half hour to put her head down and breathe. The pain in the back of her skull was pounding as fiercely as it did when her grandmother found the link that allowed Sylvia Goldberg to talk to the dead. If her colleagues caught her muttering to herself, she'd be labeled weird, bizarre, or crazy.

Sylvia's departmental profile already made her a target. She was confrontational and more than once called on the disciplinary carpet for busting lazy, indifferent cops who allowed abusers to evade prosecution due to insufficient fact-finding or sloppy on-site investigations.

As a young girl, police officers were her heroes. She read of their exploits. Officer Friendly came to the schools regularly. He settled disputes and taught kids how to settle their differences through mediation and nonviolence. Wanting to follow her father and brothers into law enforcement, the empathetic teen joined the police cadets, wore the uniform, and did not realize the subtle indoctrination she was receiving. With eyes wide shut, Sylvia soaked up the physical training and physical agility and the lofty premises of policing.

It was only in university, with a dual major in criminal justice and psychology, the scales fell away, and she came to understand police brutality, racism, sexism, and misogyny associated with policing. Going back to the founding of America and the slave trade, she learned the ruthless police tactics used to quell runaways, the policing tactics used against civil rights protestors, and finally the ways women were treated by police. She became a crusader for social justice and ran into the bricks of families… the Blue Wall and modern policing. Unfortunately, her chosen profession didn't provide resources for self-care, positive stress relievers, or a balanced life.

Bubbe, as they called her grandmother, worried about Sylvie's career choices. Sylvia was an empath; her granddaughter longed for justice and felt things deeply. When Bubbe realized Sylvie was able to talk to spirits and see with the third eye, Bubbe made sure she survived as the mysterious girl in a house of men. Together, they studied the many prophets and prophecy in the Pentitude, the first five books of the Bible. Bubbe helped Goldberg manage her gift using prayer and meditation. Sylvia was never to become a grifter or fortune teller. Even when other psychics breached Goldberg's mind, it was for knowledge. A service focus. She was a reluctant empath.

"Simmons, have some guys pick up the neighborhood cockroach, Amal, in an unmarked car. I need to talk to him." Her informant resembled an aged version of Theo's friend Cockroach from *The Cosby Show*. He was into drugs and a gang member who pled down in the original Hoskins's case. The police flipped him into an informant.

Amal was a useful tool in the hood. If he didn't have information, he knew who did. "Then, make a dinner run. I need a few minutes to clear my head."

"When did I become your servant?" Simmons turned slowly and rolled her eyes as she continued to enter data into the computer. Her jerky keystrokes and petulant mouth testified she was on the verge of a personal rant about job descriptions and handling your own food detail.

"Jamie don't do this bull shit tonight. I need some time and sustenance to regroup. Get me a steak burger and fries." Goldberg pulled several twenties out of her uniform pants pocket and handed them to her partner whose mulish face was red as Simmons acknowledged the inflexibility of the chain of command and the lack of courtesy afforded to officers with less rank. "Get food for yourself as well."

Simmons huffed as she accepted the money and pulled the squad car keys off the rack, pissed at having to perform another menial task. She was a sergeant and deserved some respect. But she turned stiffly and walked out of the office, letting the door bang on its hinges.

"Thanks, Jamie." Goldberg spoke to her comrade's departing back.

Once the ringing in her head stopped, Goldberg spoke, "Okay, Anna, what the hell are you doing here? I saw the medical examiner tuck you into a white body bag earlier this afternoon."

CHAPTER TEN

*L*ieutenant Goldberg, you've got to find Sugar Man and keep him alive. I want him to suffer for the rest of his natural life. Reliving the murder. Being punished. My suffering won't be complete unless he's back in the place he can't stand. He should be treated a thousand times worse than what I hear they do to child molesters or dudes who prey on old people. No end date, no appeal, no one coming to his rescue.

Anna's eruption was for herself, and against Sugar Man, She'd been too trusting. Numerous people tried to pull off the blinders. Instead, it was the eternal first date where everything's new and breathtaking. Both parties on their best behavior, trying to show the other how fantastic they could be together. No thought of the underlying reasons why either of them was unavailable or why the relationship relied on lengthy letters and fifteen-minute phone calls.

Anna's energy pulsed as she poured out her wretched pain to Sylvia Goldberg. The mom felt Turquoise's pain, too. Knowing she was answerable to God, Anna couldn't undo the wounds scarring Turquoise for life, potentially making her unable and unwilling to trust anyone other than family. Her murder would stunt Turquoise's development at precisely the

time she should be reaching out to form attachments with others unless Anna figured out a way to make amends.

"Tell me about Hoskins, anything that'll help me catch him." Regardless of the noise filtering into the room, the constant pings on her phone, and her anger at being invaded by this desperate soul, Goldberg had few resources to capture Hoskins if he fled the area. Reynolds wouldn't lose sleep over another battered, dead woman.

Samson told you part of it. Sugar Man feared the gangs, the dark rituals, and the game playing on the inside. He might be set up by the guy he worked alongside, assaulted by guards, beaten, and thrown in solitary for not paying enough protection or supplying the guards with contraband. He used to say until you've listened to the final click of the locks at night, until you've felt the darkness blanket you after lights out and heard grown men screaming for their mommas in the dead of night, no one other than another con can understand. Not even the guards 'cause they get to leave every day and have the option not to come back.

One day while working in the emergency room, I got a call from a prison guard. He introduced himself and insisted, "Yo boy out of money. If you don't make a deposit today, I can't guarantee his safety." I couldn't leave the emergency department without getting a reprimand or possibly getting fired. I paid a premium for the time delay. I didn't know two other women were also putting money on his book.

"Did you tell anyone you were shaken down by a guard for money?" Abuses continued in part because of women like Anna. Holding down her man. Accepting abuse. Accepting temporary solutions for long-term problems.

I watch MSNBC weekend television where they go behind the scenes at different types of prisons around the country. I was figuring out what goes on behind prison walls. I was trying to understand how to support him. Sugar Man swore he wanted a new start, taking care of us, joining the church. I was in my prayer closet every night, praying for him, begging God to deliver him from the lion's den. It seems like I was praying for him when I should have been asking God to show me His will for my life.

"They let him out a year early for good behavior." Goldberg reminded her. A year off for paying protection, for not getting in fights, and for working. Prisons operate like William Golding's novel, *The Lord of the Flies*. Survival of the fittest. Mob rule. Roll over and do what you must do until you get a release date.

That was snarky, Goldberg. Hunger, overwork, and irritated at being the unwilling host to this restless spirit. Her feelings didn't compare to what was going on at the medical examiner's office while she inspected the lifeless body of Anna Scott. She had vivid images of what the ME would find. Further evidence to convict this lily-livered bastard and send him back to Ionia State Penitentiary? At times like this, Goldberg wished Michigan still had the death penalty and there was a cure for her second sight.

"What were his plans?" Goldberg couldn't get sidetracked in the trivia. She and Simmons had to gain insight into the mind of a killer. Focus on the evidence and where it leads. Get him off the streets. It was the only way to rid herself of this unwanted Anna Scott.

He snapped cause his baby mama wasn't holding him down. That's why God brought me into his life. I ate up the lie. I assured him God always has a ram in the bush. He musta been laughin at me this whole time. Oh yeah, first, he was supposed to go and see his kids.

"Did you ever meet the ex or talk to her during the last two years?" Sylvia realized the ex might take Hoskins in and hide him for a while. Women who loved convicts didn't see the man's flaws as the rest of the world saw them. Instead, they focused on their concocted image of husband, boyfriend, children's father, provider, or lover.

Nope. Sugar Man alleged all they had was two kids in common.

"After he saw his children, what then?" Maybe there were some leads she could glean from his pre-release pleas, including what happened to derail him. Based on Samson's tale, this guy was a lightweight and without back-up, liable to make fatal mistakes.

Get revenge on the Battle Creek crew who ran and left him to take the fall. Go after the men who accepted plea deals and blamed everything on him.

Goldberg rubbed her eyes, pushing Anna to the back of her mind, as Simmons sauntered in, still annoyed. She set the bags of food on the desk, lifting out the sandwiches. The smell of steakburgers and onions reminded Goldberg how hungry she was. Goldberg reached for the brown bag. They might as well get this show on the road. "Jamie, tell them to gas up the new SUV. After we eat and sort out our case notes, we're going to hunt down a killer."

CHAPTER ELEVEN

"Where are the two of you going?" Reynolds entered their office in his customary quiet sleuthing manner. The two women never knew when or where the bastard would show up. He'd interrogate them as though he wasn't interrupting anything consequential. Reynolds had changed from the striped shirt he'd worn earlier in the day to a blinding white shirt, blue tie, and pocket square, making his suit appear sophisticated.

"Following up on a couple of leads in the Scott case." Goldberg lied matter-of-factly, knowing the drill. Reynolds took her case resolutions success as a slap against him. Nepotism was powerful here in this small conservative community. No one was going to outshine him in the department or become a contender for the chief's job except him. He was the first black man to get this far and no entitled woman with family connections on the force was leapfrogging over him.

"Shut it down, Lieutenant. The department isn't authorizing overtime for the Scott case." Reynolds stared at her, his beetled brows standing out on the sides like two lines dissecting his face. His rigid posture and bottled emotions were way out of line over

abuse of unauthorized overtime. He looked the other way when it was a case he wanted to be handled.

Simmons chuckled under her breath, observing Goldberg being put in her place. Literally.

"Give us a little leeway. We can wrap this up. The perp can't get far with no money, driving Scott's car, and wearing bloody clothes. We have a list of likely places and people he'll turn to." Solid police work and Anna talking nonstop in her ear.

"Shelve it. We got an effin' fiasco on our hands." Reynolds blocked the doorway with feet spread, and arms crossed over his chest. "Jerald Dowling killed his wife." His own crisis overshadowed the Scott case. Domestic violence, writ large, was turning the town upside down. Very few resources were allocated to a growing epidemic that now touched the elites in the community.

"He finally bludgeoned her to death. She's suffered enough 'suspicious' accidents to fund a new wing at Battle Creek Health System." Simmons' attempt to defuse the tension between her two superior officers thudded to the floor as her words reverberated around the small office. Her chance at a promotion depended on her being a team player. That black mark would be replayed again and again.

Reynolds barely turned his head, dropped his eyes to his shiny black shoes and shoved his hands in his pockets. "A kill shot. Answer your damn phone. My admin has been attempting to let you know for the past hour."

Goldberg had ignored the phone pings to concentrate on Anna's case. No need to say I told you the Domestic Violence Task Force needs more people and a budget. Two killings within hours of each other. First Anna Marie Scott. Now Barbara Dowling. No point in reminding him of the reports she repeatedly sent to him and the Chief of Police that the violence continued to escalate between the

Dowlings. Thank God for computers and instant documentation. She wasn't taking the fall for this expected murder.

Dowling, the CEO of a major corporation employing two hundred people, headed up last year's United Way campaign and donated to every political cause in Battle Creek. He was personal friends with the mayor and the city manager, and the power brokers in the community.

"Why aren't you on the scene, doing what you do best?" Goldberg sneered, choking down bile and biting the inside of her cheek. Her second sight accumulated the last minutes of Barbara's tortured life, the bullet hitting her, her brain dead before her body hit the floor. For two years, she'd been the one to investigate the strange accidents at the Dowling mini mansion, listen to Barbara Dowling's tearful pleas that her husband was planning to kill her, and be dismissed by her superiors who told Goldberg to get out of the couple's private business.

Reynolds repeated the Chief of Police's words verbatim. "Mr. and Mrs. Dowling are having adjustment problems and should be left alone to work them out. Stop responding to her unfounded calls for assistance." Barbara called Goldberg directly because male officers tried to shame her into silence. Sylvia had woken from numerous dreams, screaming at Barbara Dowling's lifeless body.

"How come there's nothing about the Dowling murder report on the internal system?" Goldberg's stomach hit the grimy floor. No second sight needed to know the internal cover-up was in place, and Reynolds was in charge of keeping the muzzle on one Lt. Sylvia Goldberg.

"Not the time, Goldberg. We're a team, and I need you standing by my side when we face the news media at the press conference in the

morning." Reynolds stared her down. He was her direct supervisor. She was the first to look away.

Please, dear God, get me out of here. Soon! Goldberg looked at her department issue timepiece. "I'm a necessary nuisance because you, the chief, the mayor and city manager, plus everybody with an opinion has been sitting around for two hours, trying to figure out how to make this murder charge go away and you know it's not happening."

Reynolds crossed his arms and leaned against the door. This time, he couldn't meet her eyes. "The sister, Amie Rivers, witnessed the murder. She's been staying at the Dowling's home since Barbara got out of the hospital."

Goldberg pumped an imaginary fist up to God. Finally, Barbara Dowling would receive a belated justice. Hallelujah. The woman's life force would be vindicated. BCPD law enforcement would receive another black mark for siding with the abuser and murderer. If she weren't Jewish, Goldberg would holler "Thank you, Jesus, for your grace and mercy."

"By tomorrow morning, every local and statewide women's group is going to be out marching around the courthouse, on the talk shows, and writing opinion editorials. Stirring up a bunch of shit." Reynolds spat out the words as if he was spitting out tobacco he'd had in his jaw too long. Nasty and creating a streaming mess.

That's it. No trip to Kalamazoo tonight. More lost time. Goldberg's anger bubbled up. Manpower followed high-profile cases, and she couldn't eke out overtime to bring in Willie Earl Hoskins. The police department sold its soul to corporate interests a long time ago. "Why do you care who shows up tomorrow, Reynolds? Everything you need to close the case is already laid out. DNA. Weapon. Eyewitness. Say it was a crime of passion." She laughed like a demented patient at

the old Battle Creek Sanitarium. "The kill shot might be difficult to explain. Open and shut murder one case to me."

Reynolds held out his hand in the universal STOP sign. His voice was flat, speaking from the script he'd been given while she was painstakingly investigating the murder of a disenfranchised black woman. "If we don't spin this as a unified department, the crime reporters will pick up on the vibes. Two hundred people will lose their high-paying jobs. The city will lose millions in tax revenues. The town can't absorb losing that many high-earning employees at once."

She pulled at her frizzy hair and stared until her supervisor backed away from the angry energy surrounding her. "Dowling killed his wife." Every minute wasted on this Dowling cover-up gave Hoskins additional time to get further away. If the trail went cold, it could be weeks or months before he was back in custody. "How does Barbara Dowling's death impact the employees?"

Goldberg, you can't leave Sugar Man out there. I already told you he's raging. He can't stop himself. He's not finished. There will be others. Don't you even care about his baby mama if he shows up at her place?

Between Reynolds and Anna, Goldberg felt nauseous with a throbbing headache. Next, her vision would blur, and she'd have to suck it up. Reynolds was doing the ass kissing needed to move up the promotion ladder. If she paid attention to Anna's insistence that Goldberg ignore her boss, Goldberg could end up on the streets, unemployed.

Goldberg hit her pounding forehead with the heels of her hands, trying to shush Anna. She was on overload with the burden of bearing the woman's pain while she completed this distasteful aspect of her job. Spin the unspeakable. Lie with a straight face. Go home and drink a fifth of Jim Beam. Get up the next day and perform like a puppet again.

Reynolds continued with the prepared script. "The family trust owns the house and cars. Her family's money started and sustained the business. Barbara Dowling owned the business; Jerald doesn't have a dime invested in it. She possessed the business acumen and was running the operations but gave up managing the business to become his punching bag. Jerald doesn't own anything other than those fancy duds he wears. His salary won't cover his legal bills."

"Knowing his raggedy backside was hanging out there, why would Jerald beat her down, let alone kill her? He should have been kissing her ass and anything else she wanted. He's nothing but a high-priced male prostitute who forgot he was the trick." Sylvia Goldberg was burned out from spending hours with turds as they schemed and lied and came up with spin worthy of the Republican Party accepting Donald Trump as their presidential nominee and POTUS. "Reynolds, what's the point of a press conference. What or who is the department protecting?"

Reynolds flipped her the bird. "Heads are rolling around here. The whole story's going to come out tomorrow. Her sister, Amie is bringing in a high-powered law firm from Detroit to sue the City and the Police Department for not filing abuse charges when Barbara's broken ribs, a broken eye socket, a fractured skull, multiple contusions are all documented in police reports and hospital records. Barbara lived in fear for her life and there are voice messages and pictures of instances of abuse not reported to the police, but rather to her personal physician. Amie has an unauthorized list of the calls made to the department and the lack of response. What Barbara didn't tell her, Amie learned from the household staff and the woman's therapist. We have to contain this, appease the sister, and keep the company afloat until the conclusion of the trial or we can convince the family to keep the company intact." The man issued the ultimate company line. "Our town's economy depends on the taxes they pay and the charitable contributions they make."

Goldberg was fighting for a bone here, a little justice. This case's outcome was preordained. Reynolds and the Police Chief were figuring out how the chess pieces would be rearranged after the public outcry. "What about the Scott case? When do we get a team out there to find a murderer on the loose who is capable of killing again?"

Reynolds fixed her with a hard glare. "Scott's case is not a priority. The killer can't get far. He'll show up eventually, and we'll nab him."

Goldberg bowed her head. She scribbled notes on the Scott file, stapled the pictures of a dead Anna on the living room floor, and Hoskins' prison mug shot to the cover and pinned it to her already overloaded, unsolved murder board. One more face she'd have to look at every day when she and her hot coffee entered, sat down, and booted up her computer. So much for "Justice for All".

Sorry, Anna. In modern policing, money eclipses fair dealing every time.

CHAPTER TWELVE

This little light of mine… The song was their anthem. Anna hummed the words as she opened Turquoise's jewelry box, warding off the dark spirits in her used to be home. Turquoise sang and danced to the words from the time she was a toddler. In church. In Sunday School. And the locket with their pictures cemented the Mother and daughter bond. Police tape and locked doors couldn't keep her out of here. She must let Turquoise know her mommy was still protecting her.

But the hatred, the darkness was here to. That's why she needed Goldberg's help to find Sugar Man. His evil overpowered her as it had on Thursday morning. Better get out of here while she could. Anna wanted to go to Heaven, to be enfolded in her mother's arms again. She didn't want to get trapped in limbo forever or wind up in hell.

Time to go home to my daddy's house.

Goldberg had kicked Anna out of her head by singing the Jewish lullaby "Sleep my little one. Sleep without worry or pain" repeatedly while she processed the lies about Barbara Dowling's death. The police department was less than two miles away from the Washington Heights neighborhood Anna grew up and where her father still lived.

Lee Roy graduated from Battle Creek Central High School, spent two years in the army, and forty years working on the assembly line at the cereal company.

Lights were on in the immaculately maintained brick exterior of the two-story, five-bedroom Victorian house. Furniture purchased thirty years ago when her parents bought the house looked the same way it did when she was growing up. The family handled the furniture with care because her mother picked it out. Lee Roy mowed the front lawn and oversized backyard every weekend in spring, summer, and fall; trimmed the weeds and tended to the flowers. If the weather were fifteen degrees warmer, the yard would have been overrun with visitors paying their respects to Anna while overhead lights twinkled, music blared, and the smell of home cooked foods brought in by neighbors and friends permeated the air.

Lee Roy had offered to renovate the home's basement into a separate apartment for her and Turquoise when she told him she was buying the house in Harper Creek. The single mother wanted her private space to raise her daughter instead of absorbing Turquoise into a communal family with three mothers and a doting grandfather. So, she insisted on moving them both away, having no idea what awaited her down through the years.

Turquoise, look around you. See my light. It'll comfort you and remind you that I'm with you always. I love you, baby girl.

Turquoise sensed her mother's presence in Lee Roy's bedroom, a room filled with the king-sized bed Anna and her sisters slept in for months following their mother's death.

"Mommy, mommy." The little girl's eyes were almost swollen shut as Turquoise turned from side to side finally finding the twinkling light hovering over the gold locket on her pillow. Her hands grabbed

it and unlocked it. Tears flowed as she touched her mommy's face reverently.

The pre-teen stopped sniffling and went to sleep as her mother hovered around her, pulsing light, and love, humming her favorite bedtime songs. In sleep, Turquoise could temporarily forget about the last time she saw Anna and the horror of it all. *Watching her baby's chest rise and fall as she slept, the protective mom longed to take Turquoise in her strong arms and kiss her one more time. Say I love you more than life itself one more time. Say I'm sorry my dream of giving you a mommy and a daddy shattered. I wanted you to have two people working together, loving each other, and assisting you through the turbulent teen years until you reached adulthood as a healthy and whole young woman.*

Anna's turbulent spirit wandered in and out of rooms in the beloved family home, stopping often to examine the contents and the essence of the inhabitants. The Victorian house's large den was a testament to the previous owner who was one of the town's leading bankers. The Scott family purchased the home after being displaced from "The Bottoms," an area in the city that flooded every year during the spring rains. The City acquired the floodplain area expressly for redevelopment, forcing black residents to integrate a city carefully designed to remain separate and unequal. When black families bought the first few gracious homes in the previously all-white neighborhood, the white families sold for top dollar and moved across town to newer subdivisions and estates.

The couch and chairs were filled with her daddy's six brothers. Their sons lounged on the floor. Paper plates of half-eaten food and liquor bottles littered her father's mahogany coffee table. Hometown favorite, Johnnie Taylor's blues albums were playing on the old stereo in an armoire that used to hold her mother's clothing.

Landon Miller, her childhood friend, was there as well. Landon wanted to be the man in Anna's life. Lee Roy often reminded her there wasn't nothin Landon wouldn't do her. Landon was a certified building contractor. Daddy joked that the new house Landon's building was a pre-wedding gift for her. She had no intentions of marrying him.

Lee Roy was breathing a sigh of relief now that Turquoise was resting. Turquoise alternately cried and yelled, demanding they go to the morgue and get Anna. "She gon' wake up askin' the same question, "Why he killed my Mama, Papa?" She wasn't dead. Everybody was playing a terrible joke on her. She was supposed to be at choir rehearsal, singing, and working on her praise dance routine. Why didn't those people go away and stop telling her how sorry they were for her loss?

Anna, her father, and sisters had made Turquoise the center of their world. She was an adorable baby, an old soul who snuggled up with her mommy and aunts as though she had a right to engage in adult chatter and add to the conversation. Never a bad day at school, in the community, or at church. Even being alone for two to three hours a day, she was a responsible girl because of structure, love, and a tight circle. The most important part of the loop was now forever lost to her.

Anna wanted to leave Turquoise and comfort her shell-shocked daddy but knew her daughter needed what little solace her troubled soul could provide. Her daughter's childhood somersaulted and left Turquoise dangling on the edge of the dismount board. How could Anna abandon her baby like this?

Uncle Raymond pulled out a handkerchief, wiped his wet eyes and blew his nose. Then Raymond drank moonshine out of a jelly jar. The seven brothers lived within blocks of each other and were a unified front. Every fall, they made whiskey. Each one set aside a few bottles for emergencies. By the time Anna was laid to rest, the grain alcohol would be history, and they'd have to make more as they grieved over her untimely death.

Raymond's twin, Robert stared down at the floor where the moonshine jug rested. Uncle Robert was the oldest of the family and the unofficial leader. "What yo' gon' say to the child, Lee Roy?"

Lee Roy shook his graying head and dropped his empty glass to the floor. The tears were gone. His red-rimmed dry eye sockets showed every blood vessel. There was not enough alcohol to dull the roaring conflicting emotions of love, loss, hate, and bitterness.

Landon interrupted. "Look, Scottie, the damn cops ain't doing nothing to find the bastard. It's all over the 10 o'clock news about that Dowling man killing his wife. The police having a press conference about that in the morning." Landon searched their faces. No one responded.

Landon Miller had loved Anna since grade school. He was a smart kid, respectful, a guy getting good grades and never in trouble. He always trying to kiss her on the mouth because he witnessed his mommy and daddy's interactions. She'd squeal and run away. In middle school, Landon pulled her long, thick ponytails, carried her books, and wrote her poems.

But Keenan Ford and the staff of the juvenile home were on a first-name basis. Anna didn't care what Keenan did. He was always clowning to get her attention, and Anna's big round eyes would light up when she saw him. Keenan stole a shotgun when he was fourteen and walked around town with it concealed under a long coat, pulling it out and aiming the gun at anyone who got in his face.

Keenan used that shotgun to commit numerous robberies and ended up in a juvenile facility until his twenty-first birthday. He

showed up at Scott's door as soon as he was released. Turquoise was the result of their explosive and often chaotic relationship. Shortly after the birth, Keenan disappeared from their lives leaving Anna, her father, and spinster sisters to raise Turquoise.

"We are going to be there!" In addition to his contracting business, Landon had served two tours fighting terrorism in the Middle East and was now a member of the Michigan National Guard. Once a month, he reported to Michigan Army Base at Ft. Custer where he continued his training.

"Look at all the unsolved murders." One of the nephews grumbled. "The police chief and the police commissioners give out the same story over and over. Cold case team never solves black folks' murders, but they settle white cases from as old as thirty years ago."

Landon seethed. "We're gonna git Anna's killer. If we let the trail go cold, Anna becomes the next statistic. And who cares. Black families band together every year for rallies. Nothing comes of it but more tears and threats." He was stone cold sober despite drinking since he'd arrived straight from paying his crew. "Let's get a plan together, sleep and start out first thing tomorrow. Anybody know his family? Which of his boys still around? After the press conference, we'll find the scum he hung out with."

CHAPTER THIRTEEN

It was three o'clock in the morning. Twelve hours since the call came in. The first forty-eight hours of an investigation were critical for finding eyewitnesses, trace evidence, running down leads and tips. Goldberg and Simmons were wasting valuable hours stuck at police headquarters until the press conference. They might as well get Amal to spill some tea.

"Sit down, Amal." Simmons pushed the informant into the interrogation room as Goldberg straddled a chair. It was better to act like a dude than to bust somebody's chops because a con mouthed off that women shouldn't have an investigator's shield. Also coming from a family of cops, Simmons' skills were undervalued until she demonstrated she could get hard evidence from snitches and perpetrators.

However, Goldberg was always the lead interrogator, the bad cop. "You picked up Willie Earl Hoskins from Ionia and dropped him off at Anna Scott's house?"

Amal, wearing shades, studied his fingernails, rocked back in the creaky chair, and refused to meet her gaze. "Sugar Man my boy, you

know. We had stuff to talk about, clear up, and make sure there were no hard feelings about what went down for he went to the joint."

Goldberg filed the information away for later. "How long you and Willie Earl been hanging out."

Amal poked his scrawny chest out. "Six of us grew up in Parkway Manor and played at Claude Evans Park." The projects were adjacent to the Washington Heights neighborhood where Anna grew up. The park was the common hang out for all the kids. "Sugar Man coulda played in the NFL. He was a beast, big hands, a strong running back."

After thirty years, this guy was promoting somebody whose glory days ended with his last high school football game. "How'd Hoskins end up in jail?" Goldberg knew what was in the file. She wanted to hear it from an eyewitness to history. His view of the story might also help Anna reconcile her killer with the guy Amal, and his friends knew.

"When he was six, Sugar Man's mama signed him up for youth football. He was a star all the way through high school. Sugar Man won some trophies and stepped outside his mind. He stopped listening to the coaches." Amal jerked his shoulders and looked right into the eye of the hidden camera. "Varsity head coach called him lazy, uncoachable and entitled because he got his name and picture in the paper after ev'ry game."

"He had swag. Brothas wanted to hang out wit him. The honeys, too. He got a couple of baby mamas." Given Amal's five-foot-seven stature, the snitch's reflected glory came from hanging out with an athlete, mainly because Willie Earl didn't allow anyone to harm his friend.

"We only know about one ex… Linda Beasley." Simmons interrupted his praise session.

"Sugar Man was living wit her when we got busted," Amal answered one question at a time. The snitch had taken a plea deal to avoid prison time and remained closed mouth about anything that might come back to hurt him.

"Who else?" Simmons eyed him closely. If Amal gave them useful insider information, he was still valuable to the department.

Amal leaned back in the chair, on safer territory now. "The first one, we called her Bernie because she was a tomboy. She went to school wit us."

"Where is Bernie now?" Simmons persisted.

"She went off to State." Michigan State University was a powerhouse for basketball and football talent. Numerous local athletes signed with MSU and other Big-Ten universities. Very few of them went on to play in the NFL or NBA. "They were supposed to go to State together, get an apartment, and take their baby. After two years Hoskins would drop out and enter the NFL draft." Amal looked past her shoulder at the block wall behind her, either focusing what was or what could have been. "He effed up by getting in the drug business. Bernie didn't come back. Last we knew, she was in Cali."

"Who would know?" Goldberg snapped. "I need a full name and a way to contact her."

"Her momma still lives in Parkway Manor." Amal rattled off the woman's name and apartment number. "Bernie doesn't even come near the place. Flies her mother to Cali to visit her every year."

"How was Hoskins when you got to Ionia?" Once Amal was loosened up, Goldberg tightened the thread from the beginning.

"We picked him up and dropped him off. Ain't heard from him since." Amal slouched in his chair, looked down at the table. His foot was tapping a fast rhythm on the floor.

"You didn't answer the question." Simmons dropped into the chair next to him, studying his shifty gaze. "Who was with you and what did you do before you dropped him off?"

"Me. Sugar Man. Louie. Donnell. Riding around and catching up."

Louie and Donnell had been mid-level drug dealers. Both were too old and too slow for the new high-tech delivery system. The younger guys were using high school kids' ability to text and meet up between class changes to push drugs disguised as gummy bears.

"For six hours?"

Amal watched the two women, wondering if one of them would cut out his tongue. Finesse was not on the table tonight.

Goldberg flipped the script. "You got a few outstanding warrants, Amal. I can call the duty officer and have you booked." Goldberg needed to get in a thirty-minute power nap, shower, change into her dress uniform, drink high octane caffeine and be mentally prepared for the 7:30 a.m. press conference.

Amal bluffed. "Day-um. Shit is bogus. You going to send me to jail for lack of car insurance."

Simmons was in his face now, snappish, and dog-tired. She smelled fear. "Show us proof of insurance. You were driving on the highway and endangering other motorists. Probably high as hell. We know you and your boys gave Hoskins alcohol and drugs."

"Aight." Amal looked back and forth looking for a friendly face between the two women. Finding none, he hooked his feet on the chair's foot bar and rocked back and forth. "Man been locked up for five years plus the time he spent in the county. We figured he needed to unwind."

"What did you give him?" Simmons' flat, monotone voice jerked him out of his story.

"Cognac. Cocaine. Ganja." He snorted. "Sugar Man kept grumbling he was gonna get payback on all the folks who turned against him, ratted him out, and left him in prison. We were all fucked up when we dropped him off at the woman's house. She not even his usual type of woman."

"What was he wearing?" Another quick question to test his recall of events.

"Jeans, blue plaid shirt. Spring ain't trying to show up. Him and Donnell about the same size. He took Donnell's Detroit Piston's Starter jacket 'cause the one he was wearing was too thin. He traded Donnell his Jordans for Donnell's work boots. Said he knew where he could get some more Jordan's."

"Why did Hoskins need work boots? He wasn't planning on doing anything requiring him to exert any effort, was he?" Simmons massaged the lines on her forehead with three fingers. "Changing clothes does not account for six hours. You are working me, Amal."

Amal's twisted his lips and barely spoke above a whisper. "We dropped some knowledge on him."

"What kind?" Goldberg leaned in enough to see the moisture on Amal's top lip. He glanced around the room, looking for the microphones and the cameras he knew were somewhere in the interrogation room.

Amal's voice dropped so low the officers leaned in to hear him. "We went to meet with the Godfather. The Godfather was supposed to bless Sugar Man for doing the time and not snitchin by giving him back his territory, a stake, drugs, and a new car. The whole nine yards." The informant's voice dropped so low the two women almost had to read his lips. "Business situations have changed."

At this point, The Godfather was untouchable. He had friends in prominent local and state law enforcement and politics. Amal, who wanted to stay on top of the ground, refused to give a hint of his identity. The Godfather covered his tracks, as well as kept eyes and ears inside the department. The department didn't have enough evidence to bring charges on the dirty vice cops. If one of them reported on this early morning interrogation, Amal could truthfully say he didn't finger the Godfather.

Amal looked worse than the kid who'd learned all at once there was no Santa Claus, no Easter Bunny, and no Tooth Fairy. "Dude spit out the message. Eddie was the logical one to safeguard Sugar Man's territory, but he got in a fight on the inside and choked another inmate to death. Eddie's over at Jackson braiding hair and wearing his pants down around his ass. With Eddie in Jackson and his second, June Bug dead, Godfather didn't see where Sugar Man could control an organization of this magnitude."

Goldberg chortled. The drug business was a well-coordinated money-making venture. Defined roles. Swift punishment. "Bet the news didn't sit well with a man who expected to be wearing expensive threads, driving an expensive car, and having money in his pocket as soon as he hit Battle Creek." Hoskins didn't have any work history outside the drug business.

"The Godfather laughed when he told Sugar Man he'd turned his business over to new folks who'd tapped the young boys and a few girls into running the merchandise. The remaining crew moved on with the new management. No loyalty in this business. Godfather explained to Sugar Man he'd have a fight on his hands if he thought it was gonna be a cakewalk to pick up where he left off."

"What was Hoskins' response?" Goldberg pressed him.

"Ballistic. Godfather kept laughing and poking at him. Even his old football stats been erased by younger athletes, and the high school took his photos down when he got convicted. We got out of

there in a hurry and drove to my place." Amal stated. "Most of the old crowd is chillin' and tryin to be legit. Nothin for him around here with no work experience and without a backer." The snitch was chatting like an old friend now. "If you tell anybody you got a record; you don't even get an interview. There are temp jobs out at Fort Custer. They keep you up to the ninety days limit, then let you go. No reason given. The next week they hire a new crew, and the cycle repeats itself. He snorted. "A grown-ass man can't survive on seven twenty-five an hour."

"Thanks, Amal. We need you to check out Hoskins old hangouts, talk to his friends, associates … even his enemies. Ask about where Hoskins could be hiding out. Stay in close touch." Goldberg reminded him. "But first, you might want to get some car insurance before you get pulled over by the cops."

CHAPTER FOURTEEN

B efore 7:00 a.m., ABC, CBS, and NBC regional affiliate stations had set up audio and visual recording equipment in the City Council Chambers, all jockeying for the best camera placement at the news conference expected to produce blockbuster ratings… a major company executive murdering his wife. This drab room added to the somber atmosphere. Cameramen were checking lighting and sound, regulating their equipment to compensate for the old dark paneled walls and parquet floors. Rows of chairs were placed behind them for the guys with cameras, newspaper, and radio station reporters.

Wearing their dress blues and black patent leather regulation shoes, Chief of Police Evan McConnell, Reynolds, and Goldberg stood at attention as the department's PR guy made last-minute changes to accommodate the overflow crowd. Goldberg hated the uniform which made her look devoid of feminine curves or breasts. Only her frizzy hair distinguished her from the two police officers on stage with her. In this setting, she was one of the guys. Part of the command. No fidgeting allowed. Thank God no one looked into her eyes where Anna was also peering out at the crowd.

You are stuck with me until you take him down 'cause them two clowns running this outfit ain't gonna lift a finger to catch Sugar Man. This whole press conference is bogus. Why do the police call a press conference when the killer's in jail and they won't even announce my death and blast Sugar Man's face out there so the public can help find him?

"Because you are a broke single mother." Anna's spirit was a pain in Goldberg's ass. All she'd asked for was thirty minutes of calm, but Anna talked nonstop. Pleading. Crying. Shrieking and wailing until Goldberg gave it up and began drinking black coffee until the sun came up around 5:30 A.M.

Amie Rivers, Barbara Dowling's sister, and her four-person legal team stood apart from the police department brass. Five local, regional, and state women's rights groups stationed themselves around the room, holding signs including "Justice for Barbara Dowling," "Special Treatment for Killers," and "Women Demand Police Protection."

Goldberg, I remember her…Barbara Dowling and her sister!

The mayor, City Manager, City Commissioners, and City Attorney sat in the first two rows of the Council Chambers. Across the aisle from them, a group that could only be Barbara Dowling's family huddled together, crying, shell-shocked, holding each other up.

"What do you mean?" Goldberg muttered. All she needed was to be seen talking to herself.

I was working a double one night when she was brought in. Her…. That woman over there."

Her sister…Amie Rivers.

And the husband. I'm glad his sneering ass is in jail. Nurses are pressed to keep quiet about the rich people who show up in the ER. I was picking up extra shifts to put money on Sugarman's books and so Turquoise could have private dance lessons. …I've attended to my share of women—beaten

raped and tortured by husbands and boyfriends. Sometimes, even their own sons or fathers. In this small town…Damn! Damn! Damn! There's only one hospital so we see almost everyone 'less they go out of town. Get him, Goldberg, please!!!

Anna Marie…Please shut up!! I'm working.

I can tell you stories about this case. She was seen a couple of other times in ER. I read it in her chart. The time he whisked her out of there with a deviated septum our jobs were threatened if we said a word. Who would have thought it? Here I am sharing her final moments. God does have a sense of humor.

The chamber doors opened at the opposite end of the room. Twenty members of the black community marched into the chambers as McConnell prepared to open the press conference. Leading the group were Lee Roy Scott and Landon Miller carrying signs highlighting Battle Creek's fifty plus unsolved murders of black people, the earliest cases dating back to the eighties.

Black community residents knew the killers. Once the victims' families got fed up with being stonewalled by the police, individuals came forward with names and credible evidence identifying the murderers. The police consistently parroted "There's not enough evidence for a conviction."

Goldberg, in the early years, my family attended protest rallies sponsored by a group of parents whose children's murders were never solved. The families see the predators walking around, grinning in their faces. They must interact with the thugs who killed their loved ones. Now Anna saw her picture added to the posters…but she would get justice for herself, Turquoise, and her family.

Chief McConnell checked his watch, swallowed, and nodded to the department's media officer as if the interruption hadn't happened. The Chief stepped to the podium to offer condolences

to the Dowling and Rivers families, and to recite the department's carefully edited remarks. "The City and the Police Department are deeply concerned and saddened by allegations that this department disregarded knowledge of domestic violence, battery, and ongoing abuse. Our Department under the able leadership of Captain Reynolds and Lieutenant Goldberg, two decorated members of the police force, are heading the investigation surrounding Mrs. Dowling's untimely death. Lt. Goldberg serves as Chair of the Police Department's Domestic Violence Task Force. McConnell's voice was powerful, but Goldberg could hear the signs of his irritability. She whispered a prayer. "Jehovah, the room is on fire. Show us the way out."

Stop lying Chief. You got caught. Your disinformation ain't go work this time. Anna eyed the chief, taking note of his clenched hands, sturdy legs locked at the knees and flush creeping up from the neck to his face. The chief was in a no-win solution, and it looked like her folks were here to disrupt the show. Wait until my death gets reported.

"Until the facts are sorted out, Jerald Dowling will remain in the county jail where he is on suicide watch." McConnell looked in the direction of Barbara Dowling's huddled family and couldn't meet their accusatory looks. "Mr. Dowling is genuinely remorseful and says Mrs. Dowling's death was a regrettable accident."

"How is a kill shot an accident?" Joye Nelson, the *News'* reporter, yelled out. Nelson fixed the chief with her earnest sherry-colored eyes. A strident African-American woman, she did her homework, used unimpeachable but clandestine sources while refusing to back down in the face of controversy. Anyone with half a brain knew the leaks were coming out of the police department.

McConnell searched his brain trying to figure out who was leaking information to Nelson. When he figured out who was aiding her, that person was getting fired. He droned on for several minutes, saying nothing and then opening the press conference up to questions.

Anna studied the eyes of the local crime reporter, Trent White, waiting for the sound of his smug voice. White profiled victims of unsolved murders, whether criminals or innocent bystanders. His influential writings pricked the conscience of the small town. He was a crusader who desperately desired to get picked up by a broader market. If White knew about her murder's cover-up, he'd put some passion into her case and get some attention from the Detroit press which would open this case up statewide. Get these folks off their asses.

White was primed to get a statement from Amie Rivers. "Ms. Rivers, what happened to your sister?"

Amie Rivers folded her arms across her chest and cleared her throat. She spoke directly to White, giving him time to record each syllable. "My sister was murdered in cold blood by the same coward who abused her. The police department covered up years of Jerald's mistreatment. McConnell and the department are criminally liable in her death." Amie Rivers faced McConnell directly.

A purple haze moved from the top of the chief's white uniform shirt to his freshly cut snowy hair.

"If this sorry excuse for a police department had acted on Babs' 9-1-1 calls..." Amie accused. Her eye sockets were dry and spitting fire.

Chief McConnell put his arm on Amie's elbow.

She jerked away. "Jerald's lack of remorse got so bad I began snapping phone shots of my sister's wounds. Babs loved the sorry s.o.b. She begged me not to tell our parents. Babs didn't want Jerald to get booted out of the company."

Amie's lawyer gripped her other elbow, shushing her. He spoke directly to White, "My client and her family are grieving this senseless

death. While nothing can bring back Babs, the family wants Jerald Dowling held responsible to the full extent of the law, including a financial penalty for dereliction of duty. They also want the Police Department to accept its responsibility and blame for looking the other way when credible bruises, witness statements, and broken furniture demonstrated evidence of domestic violence and aggravated assault." He paused to clear his desert-dry throat.

Anna counted to twenty. When are they gonna tell the public I was murdered yesterday, too? There was nothing on the early morning news shows or on the police scanners. Look at my daddy. He's bout to have a heart attack listening to the police covering up another murder while acting like nothing out of the ordinary happened to me.

Amie's lawyer threw a live grenade into the proceedings. "This morning, we filed a case with the U.S. Attorney General, to investigate the civil rights violations in the Dowling case. Barbara Dowling's civil rights were trampled on by the City and the police department who accommodated a known abuser."

If the public knew the money and time being spent on the Dowling case while deliberately suppressing the Scott murder, McConnell and Reynolds would be fired. Immediately! Damn! Anna wasn't the only restless spirit out there.

Lee Roy Scott pushed his way to the front of the room. The cameras focused in on Lee Roy Scott marching to the front of the room followed by his supporters, one of whom carried pictures of Anna and the words: **MURDERED! Who cares?**

Lee Roy shouted to the lawyer. "My family wantta join that civil rights case you jes filed. My daughter, Anna Marie Scott, was murdered yesterday, too. The police won't open an investigation even though I told them who murdered her." Scott shook his fist at Reynolds until the captain dropped his head.

Anna screamed, the sound reverberating in Goldberg's skull.

Uncle Raymond barked at McConnell and the officers, "This sorry excuse for a cold case team never solves black folk's murders. If we let the trail go cold, Anna becomes the next statistic. And nobody up there on that stage cares. The cops ain't gonna do nothing. We demand justice for my niece."

Trent White and Joy Nelson jumped up at the same time…heading for Lee Roy's side. Trent yelled, "Chief McConnell…we demand answers. Is it true another black woman was murdered yesterday? There's been nothing reported on the scanner, your website, or to the newspaper's crime desk."

Reynolds quivered with anger, speaking to Goldberg out of his side of his mouth. "Did you set me up? How did Scott just happen to show up here?"

Goldberg's smirk was condescending. "That was karma. Your media staff wired the press release information to the local television stations. Maybe he heard it from your official sources. Can I be invited to your meeting with the City Manager. He's headed this way." Goldberg tipped her hat in a small salute to the City Manager. Sometimes the cards aligned without her personal intervention. "We could have been closing the Scott case right now if you'd let us go to Kalamazoo last night." She knew she was in deep shit but didn't care. The stars were aligned in her favor for one moment.

CHAPTER FIFTEEN

Turquoise sat up in her grandfather's bed, listening to music through her earbuds and looking through an old picture album she'd found in the carved armoire. Her head was stuffy from the tears she'd been crying since yesterday. Up here, she felt her mother's aura even though the sensations came and went. Besides, the adults hushed their voices whenever she entered a room. She was old enough to know they were discussing who killed her mommy and why. Then they'd look at her with a mixture of pity and unease.

There was a knock at the door as her grandfather opened it and escorted Afeni, her best friend, into the room Afeni, with kinky brown coils, long skinny legs, braces on her teeth and an open smile, being here helped push back the tangled emotions Turquoise was experiencing and gave her someone her own age to talk to.

Grandpa told her, "Afeni's gonna help you with the dance steps you missed on Thursday night. She don't want yo to fall behind the group." He walked out leaving the bffs alone.

Turquoise perked up.

Afeni skipped across the room, climbed up into the bed, forgetting she wore shoes and squeezed her friend. "I'm so sorry, Turquoise. They wouldn't let me come over yesterday, but my mama called your grandpa earlier. He said you could use a friend." The two tweens clung together, tears mingling until Turquoise pulled away to grab some tissues and blow her nose.

Turquoise twisted her hands, looking toward the door to make sure it was closed. "Mommy can't be dead, Feni. I swear she was here last night, sitting on the bed singing and talking to me. My aunties looked at me like I was a nut case when I told them. I know I heard her singing and she gave me this before she disappeared." Turquoise pulled her necklace out of the neck of her shirt.

Afeni examine the necklace because she'd seen it before around Anna's neck. The friend wrapped her arm around Turquoise's shoulder, consoling her. "My grandma says the dead know what the living are doing. Any my grandma doesn't lie. Your mommy's always been with you. Remember how your mommy came to all the Thursday night practices and drove us to Tony's Chop Suey afterward when she didn't feel like cooking."

Their memories of shared Crab Rangoon and tongue-burning hot peppers in Kung Pao Chicken bonded them. Afeni smiled. "I believe your mommy can still see you and she's gonna make sure you're okay." She leaned over to kiss Turquoise's cheek.

"I'm not a baby. They won't tell me what's going on." Turquoise swiped her eyes with her hands and ran them down her skinny jeans. She didn't want to face that right now. "I keep doing stuff and being distracted. Show me what I missed?"

Since they were three years old, the two girls took jazz, ballet, and tap dancing together. Afeni loved dancing as much as Turquoise did. Afeni scrambled off the bed and tapped her phone for the music

channel. They'd been working on this dance for a couple of months. She balanced on the balls of her feet and twirled in time to the music. "We worked on the new dance steps Thursday night."

A sluggish Turquoise straightened up and stood next to Afeni. Afeni moved behind her friend, positioning Turquoise's hands in the act of prayer. "Oh, and we're getting new costumes. Earlier this year we got some new girls, plus everyone has grown. First Lady's going to take your measurements at the church on Sunday."

Turquoise slumped against a dresser, pain filling her chest cavity. "I'm not sure I'll be there. My church clothes are still at my house." She pulled at the too tight tee-shirt and sweats she'd found in one of the drawers where she stashed clothes when she stayed over. "The police won't let us back in … it's a crime scene. Papa told the aunties I can't go to school or anywhere until after the funeral. Even then, we don't know what's gonna happen until they catch the killer."

"You can wear some of my stuff till…" Afeni hugged her best friend and swiped at her tears. The girls were nearly the same size. "I'll pick up your school assignments and bring them over. We can do the work together."

Turquoise fell back on the bed weeping uncontrollably.

Afeni shook her out of it. "We share anyways." Afeni was strong and used to being in charge. "I'm so sorry, Turquoise. The other girls wanted to come with me, but your grandfather said it was too soon."

"I'm glad it was just you. I can't talk about this with everybody. I don't want the family to think I'm crazy for saying my mama was here last night." Turquoise shook her long braids over her shoulder. "Turn on the music. Let's practice before your mama comes back."

Afeni turned the tape to instrumental music. The two friends stretched for five minutes as they'd been taught, loosening up their muscles and concentrating on the message in the music. Afeni

morphed into the teacher. "Lift your head, Turquoise. Stay balanced. The new moves work better if you don't look down at your feet."

Turquoise complied, holding herself in the position as if their dance teacher were giving the instructions. Afeni's authoritative voice wafted around her, "Imagine yourself wearing a long flowing white dress over your leotard. You gotta be smooth, so you don't get caught up in the fabric and fall. The ballet slippers will help, too." After Afeni demonstrated the new moves, the two girls practiced the new moves five or six times and then the twirl until Turquoise declared, "I'm ready for the music."

Afeni pushed the button on iTunes. Tremaine Hawkins' *I Never Lost My Praise* spilled out into the room. The sad words evoked pictures of Turquoise's mommy in heaven, and Turquoise struggled to keep her focus on dancing. Turquoise swayed in time to the music, letting the tragic lyrics wash over her.

The dancers transitioned to the intricate moves the praise team had learned over the past several weeks. A few minutes in, Turquoise tentatively tried the new dance steps Afeni had taught her. Her right foot was not firmly planted, and her body wasn't fully aligned to begin the twirl. Turquoise's foot caught on the loose threads of the area rug, and she overbalanced, twisted her right leg, and fell to the floor.

Anna slid under her daughter's twisted leg, guiding it to a softer landing rather than the bone-shattering impact the frightened girl expected. The haunting lyrics were too much for Turquoise so soon after the loss of her mother. Every word of Tremaine's Hawkins powerful song about losing s loved one was another knife wound in her child's heart. Turquoise dissolved in fresh tears, rubbing her injured leg.

Afeni screamed as Turquoise hit the floor. Melany rushed into the room and saw Turquoise of the carpet, her leg twisted in an awkward pose. She knelt beside her niece. "Did you break your leg?"

Turquoise shook her head and moved her leg. It was painful, but it wasn't broken. "My mommy cushioned my fall. She's not gonna let anything hurt me." She wrapped her arms around her aunt's neck and wept.

Kerri stood in the doorway, shaking her head. "Ghosts! Spirits! Anna, what were you teaching that child?"

CHAPTER SIXTEEN

The hours following the press conference were a whirlwind of accusations and counter punches between McConnell, Reynolds, and Goldberg. Reynolds tried to lay the blame on Goldberg until the aggravated lieutenant laid out the previous day's scenario, complete with her request to proceed and his immediate push back. When the women's advocate refused to back down or accept responsibility for the Scott fiasco, McConnell and Reynolds finally left to meet with the mayor and City Manager alone.

As a parting shot, McConnell directed Goldberg to take the lead on the Scott case. "Make it your top priority."

Goldberg rapped on the door of the Victorian house, thinking this is what redlining looks likes. Over the last twenty years, the historic neighborhood had fallen into disrepair because land values plummeted when the white residents fled. The banks devalued the property when blacks bought the stately old houses. The neighborhood plummeted into three categories—still pristine Victorian Era homes, run-down homes of the same era, and grand homes split into apartments. Recently, a fourth type was added: brand new homes built by HUD to fill in lots left by dilapidated dwellings the City

demolished. Adjacent to the family homes was Parkway Manor, a subsidized housing project.

Lee Roy opened the door and squinted his red eyes at the lieutenant. "Didn't we just talk?" He was annoyed and holding himself together with cheap wire.

Goldberg and her partner showed their badges. "Mr. Scott, we're sorry to intrude on your grief, but we have a few more questions."

"Come on in." Lee Roy stood aside to usher her into the foyer. "First quiet moment I've had. My oldest daughter, Kerri, took my granddaughter out shopping for some clothes. The police wouldn't let us back in Anna's house to get her personal belongings or insurance papers." He swiped at his face. "My other daughter, Melany and a couple of my brothers are over talking to the funeral director. We have no idea when the police examiner gonna release the body."

Goldberg knew rattling off the facts would help settle him down before the real questioning began. "Your daughter's body will be released in a couple of days. The crime scene is active. We have to comb through everything at the house even though it seems like he was only in the living room. Anna's cell phone is missing and the phone company's working with us on tracking to see if he calls anyone. It will also ping on towers and give us a clue which way he's headed. Her purse is still at the house. We put alerts on her credit cards in case he took them and left the purse behind."

"Anna kept a low limit card in the car for gas and oil. Since he stole the car, he probably rummaged around in the glove compartment." With his first questions answered, Lee Roy allowed them to enter.

Lee Roy directed Goldberg and Simmons into the sunroom. "Sit down." The spring weather was unseasonably cold and damp, but the sun offered strong light. Coupled with the floral tributes,

plants, and comfortable furnishings, the room distracted them from the overcast weather outside.

Simmons made a notation on her tablet and clicked a button, probably relaying information to a team member.

"Mr. Scott, what do you know about Anna's relationship with Willie Earl Hoskins?" Goldberg asked the questions while Simmons recorded the answers in a police issue notebook and listened for clues in the conversation.

"Been goin on for over two years." Lee Roy mumbled through his hand. "Up till three months ago, Anna was planning on goin to the parole hearing and tellin them people he could be paroled to her house. We all kept saying open yo' eyes, but she was too caught up in the fantasy she created." He shook his greying head.

I shoulda listened to you, Daddy. I'm not like my sisters. Living at home, dating a different man every year. I wanted what you and Mama had. Forever. Even though she's been gone a long time, you still love her. You keep her alive in this house and in our lives.

"Did Anna know him before he went to jail?" The sun coming into the room soaked into Goldberg's tired back and shoulders. These cases were more complicated than she wanted to know sometimes. Until the case was resolved, Anna would be an unwelcome house guest in her head.

Lee Roy snorted, rolled his eyes to the ceiling. "OG almost fifty years old. He been a thug all his life. Before he went to jail, he walked around in three-piece suits, drove a pimped-out ride, and had a bunch of runners. He wouldna wanted a Christian woman like Anna."

Hoskins was already in jail when Goldberg joined the BCPD after graduate school. She didn't have much Intel on him. The department was lax on domestic violence. The women members on

the City Commission pressed for a strong female law enforcement officer to head up a task force.

Lee Roy looked over at a smiling family portrait of him, his daughters and granddaughter. "I tried my best to keep her and her sisters away from men like him. Her baby daddy, Keenan Ford, was in and out of juvie until he was twenty--one. Still no good. Never so glad to see a man get in the wind."

Goldberg looked around the room as she internalized Lee Roy's musings. The Scotts' home carried the pride of ownership, maintained with reverence for turn-of-the-twentieth-century architecture. Clearly, Lee Roy Scott's family home was an oasis in an area that was losing the battle with blight. "Anna didn't know Hoskins before he went to prison, but I used to see him around the neighborhood in his swanky car. He sponsored sports programs and gave money to a lot of old people. He paid for them to look the other way when his guys were dealing in the light of day and not call the cops. Those people didn't want to be around drug dealing, but they needed money. Once the Social Security check was spent, there's a lot of months left over."

That's what Keenan did as well. He was not all bad. He used drug money to finance good things for the community. I couldn't say that to Daddy.

"How'd she meet Hoskins?" Goldberg redirected the conversation.

"First Lady Watson runs a prison ministry outta the church. I blame her lyin', scheming ass. If you want some Intel about Willie Earl Hoskins, ask her. Sugar Man got the hook-up through her brother." Lee Roy blew his nose with a tissue, wiped his eyes, and stifled a sob. "While you at it, ask her why her murdering, drug dealing brother Brady Johnson's serving a long sentence in Ionia Prison. She'll get rocks in her mouth. Her so-called prison ministry gives him some bragging rights."

For two years, Sugar Man never suggested he knew First Lady or her brother. Damn me for being stupid. First Lady always had her nose in the air, talking about forgiveness and second chances. Never declared she knew firsthand since her brother was in the same prison. I bet nobody at church knew that!

Goldberg spoke the name and information into her lapel microphone. She squinted at Lee Roy and asked. "Did Anna know this Brady Johnson was related to Mrs. Watson?"

NO! The First lady didn't go to the prison. She set up the agenda, what prayers we were to do. Made sure we packed only toiletries and personal items on the prison's approved donation list. We traveled as a group on the church bus. The chaplain always met us and took the donations for distribution to the inmates. Then we were supervised and couldn't move around without an escort.

Lee Roy grumbled. "Her older sisters insisted Anna lived in her head without an iota of common sense."

This was a huge break for the team. Maybe they could wrap this up today. "We'll be in touch, Mr. Scott. We're going to head over to the church to see if we can have a word with Mrs. Watson." Goldberg thanked the grieving father for his time and walked toward the front door, imagining what Anna's life was like while she grew up in this house.

Anna sought to recreate her parent's marriage so desperately that she reached for an illusion. Why did she invest in a fantasy when there were unattached single men with jobs? Goldberg often met decent, hard-working single black men when she worked with Big Brothers/Big Sisters to identify and certify mentors, especially for boys of abused mothers.

"Let's go see your First Lady, Anna."

Simmons looked up from a text message. "They found Anna's car out of gas on I-96 near Galesburg. Seems we were right…our boy was headed to Kalamazoo. Should we notify them?"

"Send them a description and a picture plus the girlfriend's contact information. That might save us some time."

I never buy gas until the light comes on. No money. No phone. Sugar Man didn't have a way to get a message to his boys. He probably left the car on the side of the road and hitched a ride with a trucker. That press conference forced y'all to put the word out about me. It's paying off. Goldberg, talk to First Lady later. We need to be on the highway before he finds a way to get out of the area.

Goldberg hissed to her familiar spirit. "Anna, I have a job to do. The car will be towed back to headquarters and dusted for prints and DNA. After we finish with Mrs. Watson, the car will still be there."

CHAPTER SEVENTEEN

Liberty International Nondenominational Church, a modern one-story structure set on two acres of land in downtown Battle Creek, was conveniently located to attract members from across the city. The doors to the educational wing were unlocked, and the two investigators walked into the quiet lobby without encountering anyone at the receptionist's desk. The well-maintained facility was less than ten years old.

Her office is over in the left-hand corner of the building. Knock on the door. She's in there, prob'ly rehearsing her lies. She'll try to bob and weave her way-out of this situation. Quote scriptures and tell lies. The truth gon come out…today.

Goldberg knocked on the door with the nameplate: Mrs. Lenore Watkins, First Lady, and waited.

First Lady Watson opened the door with a jerky motion but schooled her facial features when she saw the two investigators. Lee Roy Scott had showed up at the parsonage late last night, drunk, rambling and threatening her and Pastor with payback for Anna's death. Apparently, the drunk man was out of his mind with grief and

regrets. When the morning's breaking news showed the scene outside Anna's home, Pastor declared Lee Roy was going to defame them to anybody who would listen to these baseless charges against her.

"I'm Lieutenant Goldberg, and this is Sergeant Simmons. We want to ask you a few questions in connection with the death of Anna Scott."

Let First Lady know I'm here and that she better not be lying on me. Before this is over, she go pay for what she did. Anna dropped down on the woman's computer screen to read her Facebook posts. All high and mighty, givin out phony advice and platitudes. Wonder how she go try to spin her brother and Sugar Man being cellmates for the past five years. She knew. She didn't say one word.

"Come on in." The voice shook, and First Lady checked up and down the hall to make sure no one else was around.

Sceeered!! You don't want the church to know about your jailed brother and how you been funneling their money to him. His movement is restricted, and visitors must be verified. Phone calls are recorded. Are you paying protection for him or is this "so-called" Ministry a long con y'all set up to give you access to yo brudder at any time?

The woman was dressed in a fashionable suit, not something for a Friday in the office. The investigators scanned the office, taking in the expensive furnishings, the counseling and training books, and pamphlets.

"I'm on my way to a meeting, but I have a few minutes. Please have a seat." First Lady Watson checked her phone for the time while pointing to a round table with four chairs. "There's fresh water in the carafe."

The three women sat. Simmons took out her notebook. "Anna met Willie Earl Hoskins as part of your church's prison ministry... We need answers."

Lee Roy Scott stumbled into the room without knocking, sweat pouring from his face. He must have jumped in the Silverado and tailed them here. "Since this concerns my daughter, I have a right to be here, to hear yo lies." His booming voice bounced off the walls.

First Lady shrank back into the chair, cowering. Her gaze riveted on Lee Roy's meaty fists, clenched teeth and eyes filled with hate… all directed at her. Silently, she appealed to the two officers.

Goldberg stood and got in Lee Roy's face. "You're interfering, Mr. Scott. Please leave. We're interviewing Mrs. Watson." Goldberg's temples throbbed. She was ready to arrest somebody and unfortunately, it looked like Lee Roy Scott rose to the top of her list by meddling in her investigation.

"I gotta say this. Then I'm in the wind." Lee Roy brushed past Goldberg and marched into First Lady's face. She could see flecks of spittle at the corners of his mouth. "Yo betta shut this damn ministry down today cause I'm meetin with Trent White from the newspaper and then I'm taking a drive up to the Ionia prison. He slumped against the table, his chest heaving and his eyes rolling around in his head.

"I'm gonna walk up in the sanctuary on Sunday morning and call you out. Then, I'm gonna stand up in the Deacon Board meeting and call for your husband's resignation. Not finna let your Jezebel spirit ruin another woman in this church. Damn bullshit. Church ain't got no call to put women in danger."

"You can't talk to me like that." First Lady jumped up out of her seat and held on to the back of the chair. Fear and something like guilt marched across her face. She put her right hand out to ward him off. First Lady appealed to the officers. "I have plans that can't be changed at this late date."

"Mr. Scott--!" Goldberg placed a restraining hand on Lee Roy's shoulder. He jerked away with the strength of a cornered bull. She spoke in a comforting tone. "Please, let us do our job. Your interference is only slowing down finding the man who murdered Anna."

Let my daddy get in her ass. If it hadn't been for him, y'all wouldn't even be here. By the time he gets through wit her, she gon' be sniveling and repenting. She ain't stopped. Ask her about her brother. See what lies she tell you.

Lee Roy's face was so close to First Lady she turned away from the moonshine covered over with mouthwash. He refused to let go of his anger in any way. Lee Roy's raging grief erupted on her. "I don't care bout her meetin. My daughter is dead, and First Lady played a big part in it. Scott family got a good name in ev'ry part of this state and country. Gon' call all of 'em. When we get through suing you and this church, yo ass gon be homeless. Get ready. I bet yo' sorry excuse for a husband don't know the half of it. But don't worry. He gon' have a day of reckoning, too."

Blinking back tears, First Lady Watson looked to the two officers for assistance.

"First Lady," Lee Roy was still in her face, his chest a breath away from hers, "It's one thing if the women go seek out these convicts on they own. Another thing altogether when you use scripture and a so-called anointing to lead sheep to the lions and wolves for slaughter."

First Lady's mascara was running. She was whimpering, "It's not my fault." If she told or did anything to ignite a bigger mess than the one in front of her, she would be unable to defend herself. If she could keep her composure, this would blow over, and she could keep her church and marriage on track.

Anna delighted in the woman's fears and tears. This is the beginning. Don't start boo-hooing now. It's too late for fake tears. Girl, get some

tissue and blow your nose. You look a sight. Goldberg, let him keep at it. He'll soften her up, and you can finish her off.

Sergeant Simmons moved between the angry father and the First Lady and turned him toward the door. His protests grew muffled as she closed it behind him. She turned back to the frightened woman. "He's gone. Take a moment to get yourself together. Then we'll start the interview."

After a trip to the bathroom and some hot tea, First Lady Watson sat on the small sofa in her office, eyes wet, hands shaking, and composure shot.

Anna blew on the recently repaired lights and set them blinking again. She knocked over the expensive porcelain cup, breaking it as First Lady's eyes opened in shock. Anna blew a cold breath causing chills to travel down First Lady's spine. Bet you feel me now, don't you? You may not know me, but you see some spirit is at work in the room. Tell that to Delphina next time you lyin about me.

Goldberg checked her watch to figure out how long Anna's tantrum would last. "Mrs. Watson, you need to call and let them know you're going to be late. This interview can't wait."

Lenore Watson texted a brief message to someone. She smoothed her hair and clothes and sat upright in the chair. She pulled a bunch of tissues out of the box and blew her nose. Her trembling hands gripped the chair's padded arms.

Needing to finish this interrogation and move on, Goldberg demanded, "What did you say to Anna when you found out about her relationship with Willie Earl Hoskins?"

First Lady's voice was whiny. "Ministry is trying to turn sinful men and women's hearts to God, not to us. Prison ministry is not the appropriate space to look for a love connection. I told Anna to renounce the devil. Turn away. Do not put money on his books

so he can continue to get drugs or contraband, or even to pay for protection." The last part came out in a heated rush.

"Was Hoskins paying your brother for protection?" Goldberg slid the question in.

First Lady's head snapped up, unable to hide the truth. Her eyes skittered from one cop to the other. "How dare you?" The phony outrage seemed rehearsed.

Simmons consulted her small notebook. "We pulled your brother's rap sheet. He has an extensive history of sexual assault against boys and girls starting at age nine."

Lenore Watson squirmed in her seat. "That stuff happened a long time ago. My brother was a kid." Lenore Watson fidgeted, shredding the paper on the table into bits. She stared at the pamphlets in the case, studying them as if they contained the only information worth sharing.

Anna pushed the pamphlets off the shelf onto the floor. First Lady's eyes bulged, and she shrank back against the chair.

Goldberg put her hand on the arm of the First Lady's chair to distract her from the falling pamphlets. "Are you condoning his behavior? We learned his sexual preference is young boys. He killed one who was trying to escape his abuse, and that's how he ended up at Ionia." Goldberg growled, startling the woman's attention back to her instead of Anna's temper tantrum on steroids. "When you were a child, did your brother sexually assault you?"

Goldberg whispered to her ghost, Shut it down, Anna.

"Get out of here!" First Lady's shrill, angry voice dissolved in sobs. Her carefully erected lies were staring her in the face as the mysterious signs demanded her attention.

"No, Mrs. Watson. Anna Scott was brutally murdered yesterday in her home by a man she met while participating in a prison ministry you created. Ionia Prison did not seek your assistance." Goldberg didn't have the energy for hysterical, lying witnesses. First Lady might mess around and get a charge. "I am going to find out what set Willie Earl Hoskins on the rampage ending in Anna's death. He's been told no before. Did your brother pull his protection when Anna stopped putting money on his book? Did your brother sexually assault Hoskins or was the sex consensual?"

This hole keeps getting deeper and deeper. Sugar Man and Brady Johnson. I can't believe my money was goin to another man while he sweet talked me and made me forget who I was. Probably laughin at stupid Anna Scott while they were sexing it up in that cell. E'ry body was out to screw me over. You gon pay, Willie Earl Hoskins. And First Lady, watch yo back!

Lenore Watson reached for the water glass, and it slid through her nerveless fingers to the floor. She stood up, stomping around the room, muttering to herself. Finally, she slumped down on the sofa and began to blubber. "Ionia restricts visitors and phone calls. They read every piece of mail. The only way I could reach my brother after he went to jail was to start the prison ministry."

Simmons reminded her. "It is a maximum-security prison, not the country club."

"I was the oldest. I was supposed to protect my brother." First Lady's voice was childlike as she recounted the events of her childhood. "Brady was brutalized as a child...we both were. The only thing Brady knows is to use his bulk, temper, and wrath to break down other people."

Now you want to make it about you. Anna's cold aura swirled around the woman. First Lady clutched her jacket closer, her eyes wary.

"Who abused you?" Simmons pressed her for an answer.

"Our father, The Right, Reverend Johnson, was a functioning addict. He could preach hellfire and damnation while lit from heroin and alcohol. He used other women for his sexual needs. They and their children attended our church. No one in the congregation dared say a word against him because he was a known brawler.

"Why didn't your mother leave him?" Goldberg knew domestic violence occurred in all walks of life, even the clergy. She'd met men who used sexual violation, coercion, and manipulation to keep wives and families in line.

"Our father was a powerful man. He was educated at Arkansas AM&N, a sought-after preacher at conventions. He met with city officials to discuss civil rights and race issues. On the other hand, our mother earned a high school diploma but didn't have any job skills. Her mother taught her to be a God-fearing wife who obeyed her husband. After being beaten down by him, Mother was too broken to do more than submit and try to stay in his good graces. Back then, nobody cared about a woman with suspicious accidents, broken bones or bruised ribs."

As horrible as the abuse, Goldberg's empathy didn't distract her from her job of solving Anna's murder. "Childhood abuse doesn't excuse your brother's behavior or why you're enabling him to assault and brutalize men in prison?" Goldberg wiped her sweaty palms on her pants legs. Excuses. Rationalizations! Being a sexual victim is demoralizing. But to victimize others and scheme with a known sexual predator is not the way to heal.

Goldberg brushed away the angry haze to listen to the First Lady's story. "Brady accepted Christ as a little boy. By six, my dad had him preaching right alongside him. He groomed Brady to follow in his footsteps. He taught Brady everything he needed to know about how

to be a man, including having sex with him and his other women." First Lady curled into the corner of the chair; unaware she had the glassy stare of remembered horror. "When Brady came to me, there wasn't any way to help him because my father was doing the same thing to me... Can't you see, all three of us were casualties?"

Goldberg's stomach revolted. "And now, the two siblings are victimizing other people. Mrs. Watson, unless you want to be an accessory to the murder of Anna Scott, don't contact your brother."

Goldberg tapped her phone, and Samson answered. "Put Johnson in segregation immediately. I'll call you back with details and charges."

The officers stood, and Goldberg repeated, "Don't contact your brother." Goldberg turned at the sound of the door opening, ready to arrest Lee Roy Scott.

The door swung open. "What's going on here?" Lenore Watson was in tears. Rev. Watson stared at the officers. He'd seen the police SUV in the parking lot and raced inside, knowing their presence was related to Anna Scott's murder which was on all the news stations. Even social media was rife with speculation.

"Who are you?" Goldberg was fed up with men questioning her authority at every turn. She was dressed in her uniform and demanded respect.

Pastor Watson heard the censure in her voice. "Rev. Carl Watson... what have you done to my wife? Surely, you're not blaming her for what happened to Anna Marie Scott?" He stalked from the doorway to his wife's side.

"Sit down Rev." Goldberg's tone was barely civil. Anna was a demanding ghost, interfering with her orderly processes.

"Dr. Watson, please!" He didn't intend to let this female officer dictate to him. He was on friendly terms with the City Manager. One

of the City Commissioners was a senior member of this church. He'd have her badge by tonight if she didn't apologize for her rudeness.

Goldberg pointed to a chair. "Sit down, Dr. Watson. There are a few issues you can clear up for us."

Carl Watson stared at his wife and shrugged his shoulders. This situation was beyond him.

Goldberg rotated her tight shoulders and checked her notepad, "Dr. Watson, what do you know about Brady Johnson?"

The senior minister sucked in a breath, caught between his wife and this hard-eyed police lieutenant. "Brady Johnson is my brother-in-law." He looked everywhere except at his wife.

Thank you, God. Scott had left the premises. Now the pastor was up to the neck in this mess. "Were you aware that Willie Earl Hoskins was his cellmate?"

"No! That can't be true." Watson stabbed Goldberg with his eyes before swiveling to his wife. "Lenore, did your brother know Hoskins, know what he was capable of?" Dr. Watson was fearful of his brother-in-law's hold on Lenore. The man wasn't a lion cub she needed to protect. He was a predator without any instincts for looking out for his sister. It was all about him.

CHAPTER EIGHTEEN

Lee Roy sat the kitchen table reading the Saturday newspaper headline: *Has the police chief gone too far this time?* The chief's picture appeared above the fold with Trent White's byline. Below the fold were photos of Anna, Willie Earl Hoskins, Barbara Dowling, and Jerald Dowling.

The City's hastily called pressed conference blew up when Lee Roy Scott and a coalition of black activists demanded Chief McConnell explain why the police were pulling the wool over the community's eyes with phony concern for Barbara Dowling when her murderer was in custody. Scott told the Commissioners and spectators the police department refused to allocate financial and personnel resources to apprehend the murderer of Anna Marie Scott, a local emergency room nurse, whose brutalized body was discovered in her home several hours before Jerald Dowling shot his wife.

Before Friday's early morning press conference, the police department deliberately suppressed information about Ms. Scott's murder while purposely planning how to cover up Mrs. Dowling's death to avoid the loss of jobs and the growing possibility of a civil liability lawsuit.

No public announcement alerted residents to be on the look-out for Willie Earl Hoskins, a former local drug kingpin who was released from Ionia State Prison on Thursday morning. Given the circus atmosphere of Hoskins' trial, he could have a hit list of the people who testified against him. Crickets from the police department and the Chief.

The article repeated information shared at the press conference and ended with: Do we pay the Chief of Police to stage a phony press conference when the confessed killer is in custody? Or do we pay the Chief to investigate a homicidal maniac who is still free to harm other people in this community?"

The Dowling murder investigation unearthed a shitload of cover-up and abuses within the police department. The cover-up bled over to the City Manager's office. Numerous women came forward with stories of abuse, police unresponsiveness to 911 calls and police intimidation. Wealthy women found their voices, stepped up, and were listened to by the news media. Battered women accused the City's leadership of allowing wealthy and politically connected men to dictate justice. Ruthless husbands golfed with civic leaders, sat on boards, and contributed to political campaigns. These same politicians hid their shameful behavior, forcing wives and girlfriends into second-class citizenship.

Chief of Police McConnell was placed on administrative leave pending an investigation by the Justice Department, leaving Captain Reynolds in control of the department. Reynolds was a Neanderthal, seeing women as property and not worthy of any investment in their safety. To him, women were replaceable like underwear. Nothing substantial would change under his leadership.

* * *

Lee Roy tossed aside the paper to answer the ringing doorbell. He opened the door and mumbled, "Pastor, you need to leave. You and yo missus have caused this family a lifetime of misery." He blocked the pastor from entering the house. His nosy neighbors, people he'd known for years were probably peeking out of their windows, wondering what the hell was going on over here, now.

"Brother Scott, we're your church family. Listen to reason." Watson was contrite, still stunned by the events and appealing to Lee Roy's better instincts. "The church is prepared to assist you with planning and anything you need for the final services." He too looked around the street. "Please, let me come in, and we can discuss this like two reasonable men."

"I already told you and yo wife why it's not happening." Lee Roy continued to block the man's entrance into the house. "Turquoise is in there, and I don't want her to know First Lady got Anna's blood on her hands."

"What can we do to make it right? Nothing will bring Anna back, Brother Scott. Pastor Watson dropped his gaze to his shiny Cole Haans. "Lenore's heart was in the right place. God is working on her. She's not responsible for this awful act. She needs your forgiveness."

"Don't talk to me bout no forgiveness when my daughter is lying on a slab with the medical examiner and technicians trying to put her back together jes so I can bury her." Now that the news was public, the community was discussing her gruesome murder. Some folks saying her body was so disfigured she ought to be cremated.

Nobody in my family ever been cremated or considered it until the Medical Examiner explained there was no way they could open the casket after taking several days to complete the autopsy. The funeral home workers would be nauseated by the condition of my body. Few Black people do cremation. There's no place for the family to go and grieve. Keeping a cardboard box of ashes until someone can stomach picking out an urn to hold them. Where do they put the ashes until they decide what to do with them? Who gets to keep 'em?

The pastor attempted to reason with Lee Roy. "Church members are calling me asking for the date of the funeral and how many to plan for at the repast." The pastor looked heavenward as if asking God himself to intervene. "You've been there for everyone. They want to return the love with flowers, food, and love offerings for your family."

"Those who want to help has called or stopped by. Lots of friends brought food, and some more food will be here tomorrow." Lee Roy flat monotone voice cut him off. "The place is almost a florist shop with all the plants and flowers. The nursing homes are stopping by later to pick up most of the big plants. Anybody calling you is jes being nosey, looking for gossip about the murderer's connection to the Prison Ministry. But don't worry, Trent White from the newspaper interviewed me. The truth gonna be all over the news tomorrow, prolly all over the state."

"Brother Scott don't do this. Let's show a unified front through the funeral. Everything else can wait until Anna is laid to rest." The pastor gasped. Everything he'd worked for was slipping away. "People will talk if you take the funeral somewhere else. It hurts me, but if you don't want me to officiate, we'll leave the services in the hands of the ministerial staff."

Don't let that witch have nothing to do with my services. I don't need no two-faced hypocrite cryin over me. And what pastor gon say. I'm sorry my wife blah blah blah. He knew what was going on.

"Man, yo brains as scrambled as yo wife's." Lee Roy shouted. "NO! That's my final word on the subject. Get off my property."

Pastor Watson offered contrition. "We are praying for you and your family."

"Pray for your wife. The First Lady gonna pay for what she did. Which means Rev., you gon' pay for either being fooled by her or for being a part of her schemes."

The pastor turned and walked away, knowing it was useless to continue begging.

* * *

Lee Roy and his brothers met with the deacons after the confrontations with Pastor and First Lady. Raymond and Robert agreed to act as mediators for the hastily called meeting in Lee Roy's dining room.

"Come on Brother Scott. We don't want to split the church. Scotts have always been members of Liberty Nondenominational Church, way before we moved to the new building and Watson developed all these new ministries. Deacon Rivers spoke for the deacons. "The deacons are gonna stand with you to make sure these cops get the cooperation they need to do their jobs." Deacon Rivers prided himself on being even-handed. "And we're gonna uphold the pastor until there's proof he was involved directly or indirectly in Anna's murder."

The other three deacons nodded at these two statements. They'd been getting phone calls, and the people wanted their church to survive if only to pay off the remaining balance on the new structure. The deacons reaffirmed, "The pastor won't be preaching, and neither he nor First Lady will be in the sanctuary during the services."

Divided loyalties, I say. First Lady's his wife...you know he gon take her side. Fine by me. When it all comes out, he won't be able to show his face at the Ministerial Alliance meetings.

After an hour of wrangling, the men shook hands and agreed on the date and time for my services at the church.

CHAPTER NINETEEN

One tipster blurted out that the men who picked up Hoskins hung out at Par IV. Now, Landon was hunched over the warm beer the bartender set in front of him over an hour ago. He'd ordered and eaten some Hennessey infused buffalo wings to keep the guy away from him. Hanging out with Lee Roy and his brothers was gonna ruin his stomach. All they ate was greasy fried foods and washed it down with moonshine. He knew how they felt. If they didn't stay a little drunk, they were liable to do severe damage and end up in jail themselves.

Landon turned around and saw a new face staring at him with wide open eyes. "Anna?"

He's gonna get away with it if you don't stop him.

His heart sank to the bar counter. He was here to do a job. He didn't need her big eyes staring at him. Landon wanted to strangle her, but she was already dead. He'd believed she'd finally get it together. When Lee Roy said she'd finally wised up, he thought he'd give her a little time, then ask her out again. Tell her he loved her and wanted

to be her protector. The laugh was on him but sitting on a rickety bar stool she rolls in and speaks to him like it's an everyday conversation.

He loved Anna, and he was tired of her foolishness. He was ready to be married and have a couple of kids before he was too old to play with them. This last scheme to shack up with Hoskins convinced him that Anna's fixation with bad boys wasn't over. Landon knew the ex-drug lord by reputation when he ran the drug trade before going to prison. Some of Landon's crew were his customers. A couple ended up in rehab, and several others were fired after failing drug tests required to qualify for federal construction contracts.

Landon was fed-up with the neighborhood deterioration, open-air drug dealing and gun violence claiming too many innocent lives. He wanted a new start. He worked double and triple shifts on the home building crews and saved his money. Landon lived with his mother until she moved to Kansas City to live with her sister, convinced the two widows could help each other out. He'd designed and was building a house for himself in the City's newest upscale neighborhood.

All around him, house music pumped through the expensive sound system while couples stepped, flirted, and sampled the lard infused fried chicken wings, meatballs, fish, potatoes, and cheese balls. Not a celery stick or carrot in sight. The vegetables were the first to disappear from the buffet the owner set out to keep people imbibing on Saturday night.

The mirrored window at the bar allowed Landon to see every person entering the storefront bar which transitioned into a restaurant and dance floor in the back. The locked rear door kept folks from sneaking in through the rear entrance to avoid paying the cover charge. As a compromise with the fire department, the double door

in the back room could only be opened from the inside for easier egress in case of fire or emergency evacuation.

The man Landon was looking for hadn't shown up yet. But Landon knew he was on his way. While he waited, he ear hustled. Anna's killing, charges of racism against the police for the stunt they pulled on Friday, and Sugar Man's whereabouts were in everyone's mouth.

A local gambler shot off his mouth. "We gotta find us some church girls. Quiet. With a good job. No one woulda guessed Anna Scott was hooked up with Sugar Man. With the doctors, male nurses, and other professional men over at the hospital, a pretty woman didn't need no jailhouse trash."

His buddy snorted. "There's a lot of freaks out there. Give 'em a taste of the good wood and they open their wallets and homes to you."

Landon's knuckles tightened on the edges of the bar. He was tempted to smash their throats, but he stayed focused. Several years ago, Landon took his savings and started his own home construction company. Scattered throughout the different sections of the bar were his employees. Guys he could depend on to carry out the plan. The first step was to roll up on the guys who took Hoskins to Anna's house. Afterward, find Hoskins, teach him a lesson, and then turn him over to the police.

Landon's earbud lit up. "Our guy's headed toward the back-parking lot." Landon dropped some money on the bar for the friendly waitress. With a nod to his crew, he walked out the front door and sprinted around to the back, blending into the shadows.

Fury gripped Anna. All of them were in danger because of her. The streetlight didn't cast any shadows back here…a place where dirty deals were carried out. Landon, her daddy, and her uncles might be in good physical shape, They had cunning and loss and righteousness on their side. All served in the army during Viet Nam and Southeast Asia, worked

laborers' jobs and went hunting and fishing in their spare time. But these thugs beat people down for not paying $5 for weed. Other than Landon, these sixty years plus men were no match for the thugs in physical strength. If anything happened to them, it would all be her fault.

Donnell, the man he sought, was walking through the unlit parking lot which was sandwiched between two other businesses. Brandon knew the mean-spirited drug dealer who was talkin loudly, daring anyone in hearing distance to say a word to him. His crew's job was to fight his battles. "Sugar Man can't follow directions for shit. I told him to beat her down, not kill her. Rough sex. Black her eyes. A busted lip. A couple of bruised ribs. Make sure she changed her mind and let him move in."

His sidekick Louie jeered, "When a woman knows you will dole out punishment, she'll do whatever you demand to avoid the pain.

"Where did you guys learn this shit...beat 'em till they're unconscious." Landon stepped out behind Donnell, stuck a loaded Glock in his back. Lee Roy's nephew Beau grabbed Louie in a choke hold he'd perfected as an army sergeant during Desert Storm. He kept the pressure on until the man slumped to the ground, dazed and out of commission.

Landon whispered to Donnell, "Since y'all so happy to give out advice, maybe you can advise me on the whereabouts of your murdering friend and fellow drug dealer, Hoskins." London pushed the gun against the man's vertebrae.

Donnell coughed. "Ain't telling yo ass nothing. Touch me, and you'll be dead." Donnell's big talk was undercut by the stink of fear rolling off him.

"Better rethink the odds." Landon whistled. "My comrades have been all over Southeast Asia, the Middle East, and Gulf Wars. You won't see 'em until its lights out for you.

Donnell peered around in the darkness and saw at least ten men armed with shotguns, baseball bats, and bricks. He had no idea how many others were hiding unseen.

Landon "You might get off one shot before I kill you. Is Hoskins worth dying for?"

"Fuck you!" Louie deflated like the coward he was. This Glock was real, not television and it was trained on him. He'd seen guys shot for using the wrong gang sign or being late with the boss' money. Nothing glamorous about lead in your ass or dead in a casket.

"Donnell, I heard you lost yo drug business because you went soft. Couldn't compete with the young boys. Since you all in with Hoskins, how about I show you how a few busted ribs feel?" Landon threw a torrent of punches to Donnell's midsection. Each blow contained the force of a canon striking its target. Landon regularly pressed two hundred pounds at the gym in addition to hoisting drywall and wooden ceiling beams at work. He slammed Donnell to the ground and kicked him for good measure.

"And I forgot the black eyes." A ferocious punch to the right eye, then another to the left eye left the man screaming. His grunts of pain echoed around the dark alley while his buddies stayed quiet, unable, or unwilling to step up.

"Tie him up for right now. We need some information about the whereabouts of Willie Earl."

While Beau did his bidding, Landon snatched Amal by his jacket front.

"Get yo hands off me." The snitch's fear oozed out of his pores. "An, you signed yo death warrant tonight."

Landon asked nicely. "Where is he?"

"Man, you better get out of my face. Ask somebody who gives a damn." The cockroach didn't know when to scurry out of the way of trouble.

"You used to be his lackey. I know you picked him up on Thursday. He told you what his plans were." Brandon rubbed the heel of his palm against Amal's chest, letting him feel the weight.

"I don't know who you talkin to or what they smoking. I ain't got nothing for you. So, step out of my way!" Amal was out of gas, and he knew it. But he wasn't ready to give in.

Landon struck the small man with all his pent-up furies over Anna's death. Landon pushed his gun into Amal's thin chest. "I'm asking. Where. Is. Sugar Man? Lie to the man all you want, but lie to me one more time, and you'll die with the lie shoved down your throat."

Lee Roy and company stepped out of the spaces behind the cars with guns and tire chains. "Answer the man's questions…or we'll have to jog yo memory." Lee Roy's brother Russell, twin to Raymond, clenched his ham fists. He wanted to smash the weasel's face.

Amal started talking and didn't stop until he told them everything they needed to know.

CHAPTER TWENTY

After the confrontation in the Parking Lot at Par IV, Anna made her way back to Ann Street and lay at the foot of Turquoise's bed, singing songs they both loved. At morning, light, Anna flew off to join Sylvia Goldberg to keep her focused on this case. She might be a "priority," but she wasn't the woman's only case or able to get all her attention. Domestic violence calls escalated since late Friday afternoon. But this morning, Anna was headed to church with her family.

Pastor Watson's black-rimmed eyes and heavily burdened shoulders looked around the overflowing church at various faces he'd never seen before. Not all of them looked as if they came to hear a rousing sermon about forgiveness…the message he'd prepared. His deacons were giving him the side-eye, probably having read the newspaper stories, and listening to gossip spread by Lee Roy and his daughters. The reporters tried to stay hidden, but he saw Joy Nelson wearing a floppy hat in the back of the sanctuary. With these new phones, she could record everything from where she sat. He didn't need a follow-up to this morning's news story or the editorial page blasting the police chief's lack of response.

Pastor Watson raised his eyes in supplication....Lord, where do I go from here? You were with Daniel in the lion's den, but I don't feel your presence with me this morning. A man's job is to stand by his wife...in good times and bad. Defend her honor. Lord, our church is hurting today. One of our leading families is dealing with the kind of agony no family should ever endure. On top of grieving, they are hounded by unresolved questions, a public police investigation, and racist victim shaming.

Restless parishioners looked everywhere except at the Pastor. They whispered and pointed at the reporters and other faces that stood out in the crowd. The visitors and members alike were poised for the show.

Too late for phony contrition Pastor. Women were not called to be in charge of prison ministries. Ask Paul and Silas. That Jezebel spirit is about to sink another man of God.

Pastor Watson stretched forth his hands. "We're in prayer for the Scott family this morning." The choir stood and sang Sweet Hour of Prayer, Liberty's regular invitation to prayer. The soothing music couldn't compete with the circus-like atmosphere surrounding the worship service.

You ought to be praying they don't sue the church and you personally.

Pastor Watson soldiered on in the face of blatant disrespect in God's house. "My wife and this church are being defamed in the media. The talk show, radios, and this morning's lead story include half-truths and lies. Let me tell you about Lenore Watson, the love of my life."

Get out the hankies.

"You all know First Lady. She's been my rock." Watson pointed to her.

First Lady Watson's body was listless. Either she was self-medicated, or the reality of her stupid actions was finally sinking in. The church mothers surrounded her although hateful looks, smirks, and outright disbelief marred their faces. They knew the pastor was lying. Many of them had gone to him with stories of their sons who were charged with abuse. They'd asked him to speak on behalf of their sons to keep them out of jail. The pastor never thought using his influence to keep black men out of jail was sinning. He prayed for the men and urged them to stop beating their women and to get counseling. No one heeded his advice.

This morning's congregation was not in a listening or compassionate mood. Pastor Watson set aside his notes and spoke from his heart. "Ten years ago, God put it on my wife's heart to create a prison ministry. When Lenore said she wanted to help, I expressed reservations, but she did a good job with organizing quarterly church services at the prison and special needs drives for the men. She even organized a Christmas drive to provide gifts for their children."

Ears perked up, and voices quietened to listen to the pastor's tale. Side-bar conversations stopped and all eyes refocused on the story.

Tell the congregation her brother was sentenced to Ionia State Prison around that time.

"The church ought to be protesting Black men being locked up for lengthy sentences. These same men ought to be working and earning a living. Raising their children and creating strong families. Incarceration is the modern slavery. Long sentences imposed for possession of small amounts of drugs. Nonviolent criminals housed with murderers and career criminals. Michigan has the fourth highest rate of incarceration in the nation."

Gasps from the crowd who never took the time to read up on mass incarceration. The ushers passed out pamphlets Rev. Watson developed last night to further his agenda.

Some of these folks eating that crap up. Pastor Watson's lying to deflect people from what his wife did.

"My wife desired to do something pleasing to God. The Bible tells us that when Paul and Silas were in jail, Timothy helped Paul, his mentor, and father figure. That's what First Lady wanted to do. Help men in jail. With a handful of other women, the First Lady created a ministry that has gained national attention and awards from the Governor's office. No one complained when the church received thank you notes from prisoners who turned their lives around, embraced our God and made amends." The pastor mopped sweat from his brow. Beneath the robe, his clothes were soaked. He was sloshing in his shoes.

A few people clapped.

"Y'all know my wife. She's the first to help anyone in need. She spends nights with sick patients at the hospital. She mentors young women in and out of the church." He spread his hands out toward the frowning tight-lipped congregation. Few heads nodded. Most people sat stiff as gravestones.

Having heard enough, Kerri and Melany Scott stood up at the same time and shuffled across people in their pew to get to the aisle. Melany strutted up the aisle. "Pastor, forgive my French, but that's a load of horse manure, and everyone in this room knows it."

Heads turned, and smartphones popped up throughout the sanctuary.

"Your wife's hands are filthy, worse than Pontious Pilot's and you ain't nuthin but sheep," Kerri spread her hands toward the deacons and mothers' board. "You sheep, so quickly led to the slaughter. Ask

First Lady why she chose Ionia State Prison for her good deeds. We have men and women right here in Calhoun County serving long sentences in the county lock-up, awaiting trial for being unable to pay their child support." She let that marinate for a minute. "But she puts y'all on a bus for a one hundred twenty mile round trip to Ionia once a month to carry out ministry."

Heads swerved between the two sisters, dressed in royal purple garb, marching to the front of the sanctuary and the terror-filled posture of the First Lady. Two burly ushers rushed forward, and hands reached out to stop the siblings advance. Kerri swatted them away. The church's camera crew swiveled the monitors to focus on them. The congregation saw their furious reflections on the three television screens, marching down the aisle. Earlier they roleplayed about Anna.

How could somebody that smart have no radar in men? Melany had no filters.

Kerry Anne just wanted to love up on their baby sister. Remember how she always did our chemistry homework?

Yeah, she loved doing it…and she hadn't even had the class yet?

Tears streamed down Kerri's face. The three sisters looked so much alike. She wanted to be a doctor. If it hadn't been for that foolishenss with Keenan Ford, our sister would be alive as Dr. Anna Scott. She would have gone to med school. Instead she settled for nursing.

Mel blew out a sharp breath. Loving the wrong type of men cut her off before she had a chance.

When they reached the First Lady's pew, Kerri lunged for the cowed woman as the women surrounding her screamed. The two ushers restrained her. Melany proceeded to the nearest hot microphone.

Well played, my sisters.

Melany's strident voice boomed across the microphone, pricking the conscience of everyone in the sanctuary. "Let me tell you the other side of the story that Pastor and First Lady Watson don't want you to know. Our baby sister was murdered by a con who spent the last five years as the cellmate of Brady Johnson who happens to be the brother of First Lady Lenore Watson."

CHAPTER TWENTY-ONE

A glamour photo taken at Christmas was not the way Anna wanted to be remembered. An exquisitely beautiful eighteen by twenty-four-inch picture of Anna greeted the more than six hundred mourners and gawkers who filed past the closed casket. Gossiping because the coroner wouldn't let them view the body. The story's been all over the news and social media. Came here to be nosey. People will be talking out the side of their necks for years about foolish Anna Scott.

The cloying smell of funeral flowers, plants, filled the chapel. Turquoise could a put the money spent on flowers here and at the house into her college fund. Hey sisters, please take some of these flowers over to the nursing home for Auntie Armenta and her friends.

The ushers passed out the funeral programs while urging people to take their seats. People who couldn't find places to sit either stood around the three sides of the sanctuary or were escorted down the hall where music and video were being piped into the second smaller chapel to handle all the curiosity seekers who came to the funeral.

The family processed in to Jesus, The Light of the World, at the start of the service. Lee Roy was held up on either side by his twin

brothers. Landon followed them with Turquoise gripping his hand. Keri Anne and Melany walked behind their niece. The extended family were seated in the center aisle with mourners and nosy community members on either side.

"How come we can't see her one last time?" Turquoise's braids were pulled back with a gorgeous rainbow-colored ribbon. She was dressed in a new black dress with a neckline that displayed her mother's locket. She huddled between Lee Roy and Landon while the soloist sang Precious Lord, Take My Hand. Landon pulled her trembling body into his arms and wiped her face with a snowy handkerchief. He reached into his pocket and pulled out her favorite dark chocolate candy. He looked up at the chandelier; it was shining on him and Turquoise.

How do you explain battery and murder to a pre-teen girl, Landon? Look out for my baby. Be the daddy she never had.

Landon spoke to Turquoise in a soothing tone. "We're going to remember your mommy's smile and her beautiful face when she was happy."

Landon, I'm sorry ... grasping for an illusion when you were right there offering me the love I needed.

Turquoise touched the small gold jewelry. "Mommy brought her locket to me at Gramp's house. She said I could open it whenever I feel sad."

Landon didn't want to believe in ghosts or spirits, but today was not the time or place to upset Turquoise by sharing about the voices that kept popping up in his head since Friday. He'd have to talk to Lee Roy who swore he still talked to his dead wife. He said gently, "Then I guess today would be a good time to open it."

Anna paid attention to how much Landon doted on Turquoise. He'd been a fixture in her life, always underfoot. Landon pressed her to take

another look at him beyond the boy she grew up with to the man capable of giving her the love and life she craved… until he backed away after learning she'd invited Sugar Man to move in after he was released. Maybe her father told Landon how he'd talked her out of it…daddy hit the right notes about an ex-con alone with her tween daughter and what might happen because she wouldn't always be home. About Sugar Man takin up with the drug bizness again. Regardless, Landon disappeared after Thanksgiving. He'd left Turquoise's Christmas gifts and gift card at the house on Ann Street. Nothing for Anna …not even the Traverse City's Murdick's brand fudge she loved. At the time she'd had too much on her mind to care about Landon Miller going ghost.

Lee Roy swallowed down his resentment to focus on getting through this day. The grieving father was in a fugue…his baby girl murdered. He couldn't see her one last time, touch her cold, embalmed face, or kiss her. Her daddy believed in the resurrection of the body. His only consolation was a closed casket funeral. "It's not of God to burn her body. Where she gon be on judgment day? Besides we're going to bury Anna next to her mother. Turquoise needs a place to go and visit her momma."

Media cameras circled outside the church as women's groups marched with signs. They'd turned his daughter's death into a sideshow when all he wanted was to bury his daughter and begin the healing process.

Rev. Alexander Wright, the boyhood friend of Lee Roy Scott, flew in from Los Angeles to preach the funeral. Rev. Wright, surrounded by Liberty's ministerial staff, stood before the assembled crowd with an air of solemnity and peace. Thankfully, Pastor and First Lady were not in attendance.

Wright's resonant voice barely needed a microphone as he addressed the mourners and gawkers alike. "Today is a celebration of

Anna Marie Scott's life. Thirty-five years of living a rich, productive life ain't nothing to sneer about. We're not going to let the devil have the victory by focusing on or gossiping about the events of the last week. We know God has the last WORD over all of us…and that includes the man who committed this murder. Stand to your feet and let's sing *I'll Fly Away.*"

Once the singing ended, the pastor moved through the order of service until time to deliver the eulogy. "Blessed are the dead who die in the Lord. Anna Marie Scott loved the Lord … and we don't need any judgmental folks in here this morning turning your noses up and passing judgment on a woman who did good, followed God's Word, and did what we've all done…made a tragic mistake. The obituary tells us Anna was a registered nurse. She was in the healing business. She was devoted to her daughter…Turquoise." The preacher waggled his fingers at the teary-eyed preteen.

Rev. Wright's resonant voice pierced his listeners' hearts…for one moment attentive to the motherless child. Landon repositioned his arm around Turquoise, shielding her. The baby girl leaned into his embrace while touching the gold locket around her throat. She stared at the closed black casket's shiny top with an eighteen by twenty-four photograph of her mommy surrounded by flowers.

"Anna wanted a loving two-parent family for Turquoise. Tell me what the crime was in that. Anna had a father and two sisters, assorted family, and friends. What she desired was the love of one special man."

Landon's chin quivered, and fresh tears fell. Why couldn't she have stopped long enough to realize he was in love with her?

"Many of you blame Anna for wanting to be loved. She didn't set out to harm anyone. She thought she was helping lead a troubled soul to Christ and away from a life of crime. She couldn't foresee the future or know she was sinking into quicksand when she placed her faith in a broken man whose demons overwhelmed him...and spilled over to cut short her life.

"Because Anna is already resting with the Lord, today's message is for the living. My text is taken from Isaiah 40:31. But those who hope in **the LORD** will renew their strength. They will soar on wings like eagles; they will run and not grow weary; they will walk and not be faint." The preacher mopped his forehead the scripture nestled into the minds and hearts of the mourners." When you wait on God for the promotion, to increase your finances, straighten out the children, and even wait for the lover you desire… God will answer in His time and in His way."

The brief sermon soothed the crowd, convicted some, and gave the Scott family a moment to remember the Anna they'd loved and nurtured. Rev. Wright concluded with a prayer, and a song, *The presence of the Lord, is here.*

"Finally, we're calling on a few witnesses to testify to the decency and joy of Anna. Don't wipe out the things she accomplished in life, her helpful ways, her loving heart to spread half-truths and rumors. Keep those to yourself. Her daughter, especially, and the family need comforting and consolation today. The prayers and testimonies will help this family to heal. When you've used your three minutes, sit down. Know this: I will cut off the microphone."

There were titters of nervous laughter around the sanctuary. "Now come to the microphone."

When the last person finished, Rev. Wright said, "The repast will be held in the church's banquet rooms following the committal service at Oak Hill Cemetery. Afterwards, I want y'all to go home and let the family get some rest. They've still got some challenging days ahead. The best thing you can do is pray for God's mercy and justice to rain down on this family."

* * *

"Anna's home going service was beautiful." Joye Nelson, the reporter made her way over to Melany and Kerri standing at the back door of one of the three family limousines. They scanned the straggling family members stopping to hug friends as they made their way to get in line for the funeral procession to the Oak Hill Cemetery. The Scott family burial plot was near the site of Sojourner Truth's gravesite. The legendary figure moved to Battle Creek permanently following the Civil War.

Nelson spoke quietly for their ears only. "I made a few discreet calls to statewide organizations who deal with prison overcrowding, prison reform, and various abuses going on around the criminal justice system. A couple people pledged to investigate not just at your situation but the system wide issues. What happened to your sister could be happening to other women as well."

Both sisters thanked her. They were worn out from well-wishers and people prying for details. Nothing anyone said today would calm their angry grief.

CHAPTER TWENTY-TWO

*I*n the wee hours of the next morning, Anna hitched a ride with Landon and his crew. She'd overheard their conversation at the repast and decided she wanted in on the action.

After the funeral, Landon's hatred boiled over. Anna's body was in the ground. He'd stood there after most of the mourners left, watching the grave diggers perform the tasks to secure the vault and pile the dirt back in. They finished with the return of grass over the top of the ground. Yet, the scene was stark as the daylight waned. Quiet. Reflective except for Anna's insistent voice whispering in his ear.

Please, don't let him get away. Police don't care about me. You the only one. I heard you and my daddy strategizing. Sugar Man can't get far without money or anybody to help him.

Anna, you askin too much. I gotta look after Turquoise. Right now, yo daddy and sisters ain't in no shape to help her. They are lost right now.

She'll be okay for a little while... cause if this case goes cold, she really gonna worry every time someone mentions his name. You didn't see her when she opened that door... she saw me.

Landon changed into outside work clothes and invited some guys from his National Guard unit over who worked around Battle Creek, Galesburg, Stockbridge, and Kalamazoo. He served drinks and sandwiches and told the guys what was up. "We know he's headed west with little to no money." He'd posted a map of the area on a blank wall so they could discuss the intricacies of the routes they drove daily and try to figure out where Hoskins could find a hole to hide out in. A black man hitchhiking between the Creek and the Zoo would stand out. He'd also need some different clothing.

After going back and forth, one long-haul trucker pointed to an area on the map. "The County's been trying to roust a homeless camp set far back from the highway. They're set up in heavy trees and brush. Nobody goes back there. Most of the homeless people living there are mentally ill or ex-military with PTSD. They want to live off the land and be crazy. If they don't bother residents, they have a sort of truce. Live free."

"How do you know about it?" Landon challenged his buddy.

The long-distance hauler shrugged and chugged his beer. "I drive off the beaten roads if I've been out there too long and can't chance the cops asking to look at my driving log. Sometimes, I've picked up guys hitchhiking on the side of the road who are headed that way."

"You always been touched in the head."

"I carry a gun and I've got a big dog in the cab with me." The trucker had a pit bull mix. "Based on where her car was found, I say we pay a visit to the Galesburg homeless camp in the middle of the night. Maybe he passed through there or someone saw him on the highway."

"Okay. We only need three or four guys." if this mission went south, their National Guard careers would be on the line.

He picked the first three guys whose hands went up. "Let's get our gear and we'll reconnect here."

In the middle of the night, Landon and three heavily armed men descended on the camp. It was set back from the highway, but the dilapidated vehicles, batteries and transmissions dumping grounds reinforced they were at the right place. One man remained in the truck. Landon and the other two moved slowly with the use of night goggles and binoculars. These men had spent time in the military and retained a modicum of tracking skills. The rain mixed with the late snowfalls had left the ground muddy. Stealth was their best weapon if Hoskins was embedded in the camp.

Freezing temps every night for the past week added to the miserable look and feel of the camp. This place resembled the extreme deprivation depicted in pictures of Appalachia. Tiny army-issue tents were set up with sleeping bags peeking out of the flaps. Garbage wrappers lined the filthy area along with mangy animals and an air of desolation. There were also a couple of shelters with tin exteriors.

Grouped around a campfire were a motley group of men wearing faded, raggedy army fatigues. Other men and some women were wearing grungy jeans with mismatched gloves and scarves and hats pulled down to ward off the chills. Most of them sat or stood in small groups near fallen trees amid traps set for dangerous animals.

Landon and his men closely followed the noises of men swapping stories around another fire pit and a car back firing on the far side of the camp. Someone was having a nightmare, but nobody moved to assist that person.

"Landon, ain't that him over at the edge of the campfire?"

Landon used his army issue night-vision binoculars to laser in on the hunched over man who kept his head down. He was wearing threadbare sweats and a plaid work shirt. A knit cap was pulled down

low hiding his hair and part of his face. On his feet were a pair of steel-toed work boots. "That looks like him. Don't move in. Get in position around to block his escape. Then we're gonna wait for him to move away from campfire so we can get a closer peek at him."

Silently as possible, the other two men moved around the sloppy ground. Memories of army campaigns guided their footsteps to create a perimeter. They stumbled along, hearing a couple having sex in the woods, and howling noises of men… crazy… homeless…. PTSD…. ready to kill over a tiny space.

Eventually, the man they assumed to be Hoskins made his way over the makeshift latrine. Landon and his men moved to surround the horrible smelling shack. The camp didn't have any lye to cover the fetid body waste, but it was the only place for a semi-private reckoning. As the man he knew to be Hoskins came out of the makeshift latrine, Landon wanted to gag. Hoskins was bigger than Landon but slower.

Landon learned to disable the enemy in the army. He grabbed a fallen tree branch and slammed it into Hoskins' back, just above his waist. The murderer's scream was muffled by the wind as he fell to his knees. That extra second gave Landon the leverage to climb on the man's back, punching him strategically to harm his kidneys and liver.

Hoskins roared like a wounded bear and jerked out of Landon's grasp. Degrading years of prison life had taught him survival skills. He fought back, attempting to scratch Landon's eyes out. He landed several punches to Landon's ribs, but the man kept coming with combinations and deadly force. A bloody and bruised Hoskins finally slipped away and made a break for camp stumbling over rocks and downed tree limbs. He crashed into the rock fists of Landon who sprinted faster than he'd ever done as a high school track star.

The three men punched, kicked, and beat Hoskins until they were finally rousted by other men at the camp. When the deed was done, Landon called Lee Roy. The older man asked, "Did ya find him?"

"The strangest damn thing kept happening when I was trying to deliver the fatal blow. Some niggling voice in my head kept screaming *'don do it? We need payback for Anna.'* Don't worry, man. He won't get far."

CHAPTER TWENTY-THREE

An anonymous call from a burner phone was on Goldberg's phone the next morning.

Made sure he ain't going nowhere for a couple of days ... until you can get to him. A couple of guys rolled him. He's a real pussy when it comes to fighting off men. They stole his money, busted his lip, and wrenched his arm in the process.

Goldberg cradled her head in her hand. "Were these men Landon and your father, Anna?"

"No. They would have killed him. He can't get off that easy. For it to be vengeance, he must suffer. Gonna do him as he did me.

"Payback."

Settle the score. I want Sugar Man in a downward spiral. Block his access. With daddy and Landon beating down the people who picked him up, he's isolated. No phone. No place to stay. The attackers took his wallet and ID. Those wanted posters went up immediately. Crime Stoppers blasted his face. People finally on the hunt.

"I'm settlin this score. I want Sugar Man. With daddy and Landon beating down the people who picked him up, he's isolated. No phone. No

ID. No place to stay. The Crime Stoppers blasted his photos today, so he's gotta be careful of being spotted.

Two days later, an urgent message from Kalamazoo Public Safety popped up on the department's email account. Goldberg read it three times, rubbing her electrified head, making her hair resemble a Pekinese dog on his way to the groomer. "It's Hoskins! I know it!"

A railroad car worker found brutalized bodies of four prostitutes at the Mills Street Intermodal. While linking cars together for transport from the GE plant to an Indiana car manufacturer, he was overcome by the unbearable stench coming from one of the cars. He assumed an animal crawled in one of the boxcars and died. He opened the car door and found the first nude body in the back corner, bludgeoned to death, covered with flies and maggots.

When backup officers and canine corps arrived and searched every car, finding three additional bodies in blood-soaked boxcars. The police witnessed the aggression that built from woman to woman, the last one's brains resembling wet saltine crackers. All the women were prostitutes.

Anna screamed at Goldberg, "It's Sugar Man!", preventing the officer from reading any more of the message. Look at the way he's killing them! He's killing me repeatedly!

"He didn't have sex with you." Goldberg reminded her. "These women had sex before they were murdered."

He meant to. He told me on those foul phone calls before I cut him off. With me, the rage got him, and he couldn't stop it. Yo ass don't need to be NCIS to know he wouldn't get far. He's getting worse.

"Violence against prostitutes isn't news around this area. The only reason this is a priority is because of where it occurred."

Anna snapped. "This is revenge. *Them records you keep poring over for new clues say he was regularly raped in prison! He was the vulnerable one; he was overpowered back then! Goldberg, the women can't fight back now!*"

"You need to shut up, Anna. You and Reynolds are vying for prima donna of the day, and I'm not the one. I'm dealing with the fallout from the Dowling domestic violence cover-up. Then Lee Roy Scott and his posse engaged in straight up vigilante justice. I know they orchestrated that fight over at Par IV. Nobody saw anything. The place was packed and not one witness. He's thwarting my investigation in your case."

The spirit was a nuisance. Shutting Anna down by retreating into her time in the Jewish kibbutz in Jerusalem was another way Goldberg could conduct business. After finding the name of Kalamazoo Public Safety lead investigator, Brian Cummings, Goldberg punched in the number. When Lt. Cummings picked up, she poured out the elements of the case, ending on a ragged breath, "Willie Earl Hoskins murdered a woman in Battle Creek on the day he was released from Ionia. We've been looking for him for ten days. We have reason to believe he was or is in the Kalamazoo area. I think we might be looking for the same perp. Can we join forces?"

"Tell me how the Boxcar murders are related to your investigation." Brian Cummings' Midwestern drawl made him sound like a no-nonsense, by-the-book investigator. Right now, no reputable police agency wanted to be a part of the drama in BCPD, and she didn't blame him. "Then we can deal."

"Stay by your computer. The case file is on the way." Before she could hit the button to send the file, Samson hit her up on her private line.

"Hey sweet cheeks." The crooked guard was gleeful. "Thought you'd want to hear this one personally."

"This better to be good. Got a lead on Hoskins and I need to get there before we lose him again."

"Just a heads up for you. Somebody lit a match under DOC." The Department of Corrections is rife with complaints. Johnson's in segregation for sixty days."

"That's quick movement."

"Seems the governor has more than Flint's contaminated water added to his worst governor in the nation designation. Total lack of oversight. He's touted Liberty International's Prison Ministry, given awards to Lenore Watson and she was slated to receive one at some big law and order push he's on. He nor his people had any inkling First Lady Watson's brother was a murderer serving twenty-five years to life at Ionia."

"When did this happen?"

"This morning. When I reported for duty, the change liaison reported on it."

"What's the chatter?" Since it seemed Samson was ready to talk, she pressed the button to send the file to Kalamazoo without checking it.

"Keeping my ear to the ground. Cons and some guards grumbling about that ministry shutting down with no warning. The women came here quarterly, you know. So, the guys are pissed off. Especially since the crackdown extends to other groups as well."

"Samson, thanks for the heads up. I really owe you on this one. I've gotta go before my killer gets away."

"Give him a kick in the nuts for me when you catch him."

* * *

Cummings' voice was brusque when he called back two hours later. "Looks like we can form a joint task force. How soon can you be over here?" In an offhand manner, he bragged, "Captain Reynolds and I were at the police academy together. We started out together in Cornflake Capitol until I got a better offer."

She heard the derision in Cummings' voice. In anticipation of this outcome, Goldberg had uploaded the entire Anna Scott investigation file onto a thumb drive. Prison photos. Fingerprints. Inmate file. Her timeline and contacts with the murderer's mother. Now she could personally follow-up on information Amal had gotten out of people in Kalamazoo. Amal claimed not to have seen Hoskins anywhere and not to have gotten beaten down on Saturday night.

Cummings had not performed minimal due diligence. Although he'd been informed Hoskins could be headed for Kalamazoo after the murder. The murderer had personal reasons to go to Kalamazoo. "My informant found out Hoskins' mother's in Mississippi caring for a family member dying of cancer. Sugar Man complained about his mama not coming through after all he did for her. He even bought and furnished her a little house on the East Side and bought her a late model car when he was ballin. He paid her debts. The best she could do was maybe ten or twenty dollars on his commissary. That buys nothing."

"When I reached her earlier by phone, Mamie Hoskins told me she has no immediate plans to return to Kalamazoo, preferring to stay with family. She sent him what little money she could monthly, believing he'd be in jail for the remainder of his sentence. She didn't tell Hoskins she moved because she doesn't want to deal with him."

"Saves us having to track her down. These guys usually run crying to mama when they're in trouble." Cummings snapped.

Before the behind-the-bar brawl on Saturday, Amal had hooked Goldberg up with Hoskins' ex-girlfriend in Kalamazoo, the most likely place he would have gone after finding out his mama skipped town. "Hoskins had a history of verbal and physical abuse against his girlfriend which she didn't report at the time of his arrest."

Goldberg admonished the woman to find a haven away from the area immediately and not to leave any contact information Hoskins could access.

"Can you get me clearances and access to the information I need to close this case?" Goldberg asked the sneering lieutenant.

Cummings sent a text to Records and the appropriate officers announcing the joint task force for the Boxcar murders. "Taken care of." This was an arranged marriage and Cummings intended to do only the minimum to give the appearance of a partnership.

"Give me an hour and I'll be on the scene." The two cities were 20 miles apart along Interstate 94 but thousands of miles apart in policing philosophy. Kalamazoo's state of the art facilities set them up as the leader in the region while Battle Creek was building its first new public safety facility in forty years.

"Don't rush" Cummings growled. "It's gonna take us several days to catalog and get five women identified through dental and medical records."

"Why so long?" Goldberg didn't have another two days to waste.

"We serve the entire county. And these are not the only homicides we're dealing with. The Uber driver who went on a killing spree in March is still sucking up all the oxygen around here. We've got two survivors who are now able to give us witness statements. We're dealing with at least eleven distraught families, piecing together the prosecution cases, and getting justice for innocent victims of gun violence."

"What you're telling me is killing prostitutes is not a priority." Goldberg dealt with the same old shit everywhere. Police operated in black and white. Worthy and unworthy. Prostitutes were unworthy. And if race were a factor in the case, minimal effort. Guilty. Let's move to the penalty phase.

"We're a metro police operation. We have random acts of violence. Spring, is a time for college kids to raise hell because they can." Cummings spoke to her like she was a rookie.

Goldberg's acidic stomach rumbled. Best to remember this was his house. She was a guest. "Give me an office today, and I'll do what I can on my own. We need to find this guy before he kills a coed. How will that play in the Zoo?"

CHAPTER TWENTY-FOUR

"You *gotta step up your game, Goldberg. My baby's bout to go crazy thinking Sugar Man's coming back to kill her. She can't sleep, eat, or got to school. My name is still in ev'ry body's mouth in the hood.*

The unholy alliance of Goldberg and Cummings worked day and night, not going home, grabbing a couple of hours sleep in the station's bull pen, and fixated on finding Hoskins. Even in Kalamazoo public safety command, the message was clear: Get this guy off the streets as soon as possible. With two universities close to downtown Kalamazoo, high powered corporations and City officials didn't want to face public outcry about a woman killer on the loose. Using techniques she gleaned from her time at Quantico, Goldberg scoured the medical examiner's data and created a profile of the boxcar murderer.

Goldberg, get yo head out your ass. One of these cases doesn't fit Hoskins' profile. Number four. She's older than the others. No violence. Not spur of the moment rage. Sugar Man is sick, but this is not him. Something's off with the body. This body was dumped here.

137

"Either he's switching up, or we got a second killer... something shocking is going on here." Goldberg's conversation with the ME corroborated Anna's laser-like focus on Hoskins and swirled around in Goldberg's head. The body was moved after the murder. The ME confirmed this woman was not homeless. Her new dental work was expensive. I'm not even sure she's a prostitute.

Goldberg reviewed the case files again, noting significant dissimilarities in Case Number Four. A copycat? That didn't make sense. Not enough details had been released to the public for anyone to know the manner of death in the Hoskins cases. A rookie cop was trained to spot discrepancies in a serial killer's pattern. Other than her and Cummings, who had access to these files?

It's not a copycat killing, Lt. Goldberg. I don't know how you ever solve cases. Oh yeah, you got about fifty unsolved murders back in BC. You can't concentrate because you got Battle Creek drama, yo' wretched boss, and Sugar Man on the brain. Women were bein' killed over here long before Sugar Man showed up in Kalamazoo. Public Safety responds to pressure, not anonymous working girls whose bodies are never claimed by family.

Anna, shut up and give me some time to think this through. "Cummings," she pushed the intercom, "Get in here. We got a situation."

Cummings' face was flushed as he came in. His collar was askew, and his hair looked as if rats were playing in it. "What's so important about this case that you have to disrupt my work?" Cummings pointed a shaky finger to the files on the table in front of her.

"Hoskins did not commit one of the boxcar murders." Goldberg pushed Jane Doe #4 Case toward Cummings. "The cause of death is strangulation." Goldberg spread the gruesome photos the ME provided around the table. "The beating was done post-mortem.

Look at the wounds and how they don't compare to the wounds on the other women. Plus, she's the oldest of the victims."

"Fuck!! So, he changed up one time. Murder is murder." Cummings rolled his eyes heavenward as he picked up the photos she'd lined up as if seeing them for the first time. "Women!!!

"The ME flagged the differences when she sent the files to you." Goldberg stared him down.

Cummings couldn't hold her gaze. "Why are you pouring over pictures of dead prostitutes?" Cummings' face reddened and his nostrils flared. He retorted. "No one invited you to snoop around in our cases. Confine yourself to Hoskins. I'll deal with the ME."

"Those files are evidence." Cummings didn't intimidate her. After repeated intimidation tactics. her father, brothers and co-workers learned to respect her skills. While at Quantico, she kicked ass and busted the balls of G-men who wanted to pigeon-hole her as a wannabe profiler. "They tell a lot about a perp's state of mind when examining the victims in sequential order. Is he deteriorating? Is he getting more sadistic? Remember, he didn't have sex with Anna Scott."

"Hell, if I care." Cummings' face was a mask of hostility. "You're over here to get this one piece of trash off the streets."

Goldberg ignored his childish rant and rubbed the heel of her palm against her cheek. "Hoskins is disarming them. Most prostitutes carry some type of weapon to protect themselves on the streets. He's picking younger women, probably thinking they don't know the ropes. He's probably assuming they earn more money than the ones with worn heels. He's stealing their money."

"How do you know?" A thick line marred his forehead. Cummings was looking at her as if she were speaking scripture in ancient Hebrew.

Goldberg knew she was talking to the window for all Cummings cared. She fell back on her Quantico training. They were the best at profiling and tracking serial killers. "I don't bust prostitutes; I talk to women." She was here on assignment. She needed Cummings' assistance, and she knew how the thin blue line functioned. She ducked her head in frustration. She'd crossed the line calling out another police agency's work.

This cop don't care about those women. He's goin through the motions pretending to cooperate. Note to you: Cummings is the leader of this "so-called" Task Force. He didn't look at the ME's comments when this is the most high-profile investigation going on around here. Kalamazoo is his community and they, too, have a terrible history of overlooking violence against prostitutes. A few years ago, their City Commission was bombarded by women activists who called them out. They improved for a minute and then went right back to the good-old-boys' way of doin' things.

"Not everybody is a-bleeding heart liberal or soft on prostitutes. Prostitution is a crime." Her reluctant host's offensive words were meant to cut.

While you two pissin about who's doing the most, there's a killer in addition to Sugar Man out on the streets.

CHAPTER TWENTY-FIVE

"The reward money ought to be mine. How can I get it?" The woman wearing a long Beyoncé wig stood at the front desk of the Kalamazoo Public Safety Department's central station, popping gum, and yelling at the officer on desk duty.

Goldberg and Cummings came out of the office as the words "reward money" interrupted their terse conversation. Looking for tips, the *Silent Observer* was offering a $10,000 reward for the person or persons who came forward with information about the whereabouts of Willie Earl Hoskins leading to his capture and arrest.

Police officers blanketed the Kalamazoo, Galesburg, and Mattawan areas with Hoskins's mugshot provided by Ionia prison. His face was splashed across day-time television and during every news program. His pictures were distributed to the staffs at the local mission, barber shops, other places where homeless men and women loitered. So far, the tips led to dead ends. Amal and his sources dried up although the cops kept interfering with his money-making operations.

Folks smell money. I told you, Goldberg. You are gonna get their attention. They gonna say what they know in hopes of a big payday.

Pressured by her ever-present inconsolable spirit, Goldberg's eyes moved up and down the prostitute. Hips and butt... assets to tempt a man. Her Beyoncé wig worn slightly off-center accented her brown face. If you put her picture next to Anna's, a near-sighted man with glaucoma could see a resemblance. But those garish purple leggings, high heels, and fake leather jacket no animal would ever be seen in blasted her professional working girl status. The glaring difference between her and Anna was her age. This woman was in her early twenties.

Goldberg strode up next to the duty officer and put her hand out. "Hold on a minute. Let's get you into a room. You can tell us what you know, and then if it's useful in capturing Hoskins, we'll talk money." The interrogation rooms at BCPD couldn't compare with Kalamazoo's facilities. Hopefully, the newer facilities would include the additional mirrors and recording devices.

"This old gangsta tried to get me to go with him, offered me $50 for a blowjob. When I saw he was headed toward where they keep them boxcars, the pieces came together. He's the killer. I know it." Her shrill voice, still quaking from running for her life, caused other station personnel to gather around.

Shit, Ms. Whatever yo name is. You gotta work. I get it. But posters about a killer preying on working girls are nailed up all around town. Silent Observer is blasting his face and reward amount on the television. Money comes after the arrest. Even the cops warning y'all stupid asses to be on the alert. Don't y'all believe this is real? Think before goin' off wif some random man.

"Quit tripping, Fawn." Cummings strident voice cast a pall over the room. He obviously had dealt with her before. "Wait until we get you into a room and then tell us what you think you know." His harsh voice shut down the woman.

There were anger and fear in Fawn's eyes. Cummings warned her. "You know how we deal with liars. Yo' ass will end up in the slammer."

Miss Purple Faux Leather took a shuddering breath and rolled her eyes at Cummings.

Goldberg looked over her shoulder at Cummings who was smirking. He spoke to the duty clerk. "Get us a room and some water."

Goldberg's antenna went up another notch.

Five minutes later, they were in an interrogation room with a metal table, three chairs, and a one-way mirror. The other members of Cummings' regular team watched and listened in on the interview firsthand. Time and weather were the enemies now. The unseasonably cold, rainy weather had kept most of the homeless population and the working girls off the streets for the last few days and slowed down their efforts to catch Hoskins.

"Here, drink this." Instead of water, Goldberg placed a cup of hot black coffee in the young prostitute's hand.

Fawn took a healthy swig of the strong brew. She straightened up, sucked in a couple of breaths. Focused her eyes on Goldberg.

Goldberg pulled up her chair next to the woman. "Describe the man you saw."

Fawn shook hair strands out of her eyes. "He's big. About six feet tall and built with a muscular torso, shoulders, and arms. Thick thighs." She searched Goldberg's face, trying to find some sympathy. "I check out a guy to see if he's worth the effort. He ain't the only pervert out there on the streets."

Goldberg nodded. Rampant prostitution was America's shame.

"He needs a shave. Looks like he was in a fight with a mountain lion. Face all scratched up." Goldberg placed six mug shots on the table in front of Fawn. They'd incorporated a different photo of

Hoskins from the one they splashed around town. The additional five mug shots were from men similar in build and coloring to Willie Earl Hoskins.

"Can you pick him out of this group?" Goldberg needed more than general size and build to move these cops off the dime. Only the presence of an executioner so close to their central police station and carnage on the edge of a distressed neighborhood kept them vigilant. With the new knowledge of a second killer out there, Goldberg needed to watch her own back. These cops were slightly more sympathetic than Captain Reynolds, but not a lot.

Fawn's hands shook as she studied the photos. Goldberg checked her out, realizing the woman was young, perhaps nearer twenty. The heavy make-up and time on the street had aged her. She exhibited a toughness, probably from being abused, robbed, or beaten on the regular.

"That's him." The middle finger stabbed at Hoskins' photo.

Goldberg passed the photo to Cummings.

"Give me my share of the money and let me go. I got a sick baby at home. She needs her medicine." She glared at the two officers.

Goldberg shook her head. "Not so easy. Your tip must help us catch him. What he's wearing."

Fawn closed her eyes tight as if seeing him in her mind's eye. "Dark pants. Sweatshirt. Jacket."

"What kind of jacket?"

"A raggedy combat jacket. Beat up, torn, dirty."

Probably from women trying to fight back. These women are pros, not like me. They would put up a fight, trying to stay alive.

Thanks, Anna. "Did you see any scars on him, Fawn?"

Fawn bit her lip, scrunched up her nose as visualizing the face of the man who intended to kill her. She nodded. "A scabbed-over scratch down the left side of his face. His knuckles were scraped raw. I assumed he'd been on the losing end of a fight with one of the groups at the homeless camps." She shrugged her shoulders, looked down at the five pictures arrayed on the table. "These guys hang around the area between the McDonalds and the Amtrak. They fight over cheap liquor, women, and blankets. They are all crazy."

"Since you know how violent the place is, why are you hanging out there?" Cummings contempt for the woman was evident in the terse words.

"My baby got asthma. I needed a couple of hundred dollars to pay for the medicine she needs." Fawn had tears in her eyes. Another young mother selling her body to support herself and her child.

"What about welfare?" Cummings spat the words out.

Fawn shot a hate-filled look at Cummings. "Because of you," She pointed a talon-like finger at Cummings, "They took my baby and gave her to my grandmother who is a straight-up thug. She lets me live in her house so I can take care of my baby, but she won't give me any money. Claims she needs all the welfare money for her trouble. Grandma knows how to play the courts and the cops. She took Lexi to the emergency room, but she wouldn't shell out the co-pay for the drugs my baby needs."

Damn! Everybody got a story. You can work on hers later, Goldberg, because I know you will. But right now, you gotta stay focused on me.

Goldberg took down Fawn's information and whispered to Cummings, "Give her $200 out of the slush fund you keep for informants."

While Cummings shot her a dangerous look, Goldberg went to the door and spoke to the undercover and plainclothes officers. "Check out the area she mentioned."

Cummings came back with ten twenty-dollar bills. "You better not be scamming me."

The young mother took the money. "Thank you." She ran out the door.

CHAPTER TWENTY-SIX

*G*oldberg, *we need to be canvassing the area, not combing through files. Sugar Man don't have money, ID, and a way to get out of town. He's gotta surface soon, and we need to be there to catch him. With all the homeless people around here, he can blend in, keep his head down. Those people got worries of their own. If he ain't stealing or pulling weapons on anybody, they are not going to ask questions. They have secrets of their own.*

Cummings interrupted, rapping on the table. "Goldberg, this is your last warning. Keep your nose out of this department's business. One call from the chief here and your career tanks." No longer collegial, Cummings' face was a mask of hatred, one usually reserved for hardened criminals. "Who cares if Quantico thinks you'd make a great fed? Grand Rapids won't touch you when they learn you overstepped your authority after we graciously allowed you to participate in our case. Your perp flew the coop. If it hadn't been for us, you'd still be chasing your skinny tail."

Goldberg's head and eyes rose to half-staff. She needed toothpicks to keep her eyes open. She was waiting to hear back from Simmons about her meeting with Brady Johnson, Samson, and Ionia's personnel in charge of setting up the prison ministry. Evidently, he'd done some digging around after she called him on his bullshit. Cummings didn't care about the woman bludgeoned to death. He didn't care about Fawn or her sick baby. He wanted to avoid problems spilling over into his downtown area.

Goldberg, get a grip on yourself. Cummings could care less if you get Sugar Man. If you keep this up, you might end up in the Kalamazoo River. You keep thinking this is about Hoskins? These cops don't give a damn about him. They are gonna' put a bullet in his head and walk away. Your only priority is M-E! This Cummings guy doesn't respect you. I felt the hostility from the movement we arrived here. When we're done, drop a dime on him. You know he dirty. That girl feared him. Y'all need to drop it for a minute.

Alright. There was nothing Cummings could do to Goldberg unless he wanted everyone in the county to know he'd been withholding crucial information about a serial killer. However, if Cummings reported her, it would solidify Reynold's accusations that she was not a team player. If she stood a chance for an interview in Grand Rapids, aside from her other skills, contributing positively to team efforts was a necessity. Cops forgot other cops knew the drill. And the *coup de gras* — the killer was probably a cop.

"You've got a rogue cop operating out of this department, killing vulnerable women. No one in the department cares." She batted her eyelashes and gave him a demure smile.

Cummings's face was blotchy. He opened his mouth, snapped it shut. His fists drummed on the walled enclosure. Both knew this was a stalemate. He'd deal with it once they scooped up Hoskins.

"Don't insult me by saying no one connected the dots before I did." Unrelenting, Goldberg put up a shaky hand. Too much caffeine, not enough sleep, and Anna's chatter.

"Put a pin in it, Goldberg." Cummings' hard eyes with menace behind them lasered into hers.

"Nope." Either Cummings was involved, or he'd done nothing to stop the killing. "In case you're interested. I did a profile on your cop."

Cummings stopped fidgeting and looked at her, hatred shooting from his eyes.

Goldberg described her killer's profile. "Arrogant. Brutal. Kills them because he can. Judge, jury, and executioner."

"Which could be half the squad. A lot of these newer guys served in Desert Storm, Iraq. Afghanistan. They liberated Baghdad and Fallujah." Cummings hooted.

"Some officer's seen signs or heard a rumor. The blue line keeps him or her from coming forward, or they got skeletons, too." Goldberg asserted. "You tell me."

"The philosophy around here is sex-workers, prostitutes…who gives a damn." Cummings summed up the message regarding law enforcement across the nation.

Goldberg shot back. "A glorified street bandit. Maybe thinks he's back in the war. Scared shitless. So, he takes it out on helpless women."

Cummings bit back a curse as he punched the wall behind her. "Do you want a slander lawsuit against you or Battle Creek PD?"

"Slander? Seriously!! I created a profile. I've named no one." Goldberg looked him up and down." How many other people must be murdered before some slick Gazette news reporter gets a whiff of this story? You'll have the state and the feds all over Kalamazoo."

"Shut it down, Lieutenant. You're a guest here."

"So, you'll condone murder against women as long as you don't have to look at one of your own."

CHAPTER TWENTY-SEVEN

Too many personnel were working around the squad's open area for Cummings to throw Goldberg through the plate glass window. He tamped down his anger. The woman was lethal. Quantico and Reynolds both had verified her skill level. She kept her weapon close at hand, and if he tried to detain her, she'd probably take him down.

Cummings rage was at 100 as he scrounged around in his desk for the phone he'd cloned when he found out one of his officers was banging his wife. Who knew when Cummings would get a chance to dirty up the deceptive s.o.b. and fuck him over? Until then, he used this burner when he needed anonymity. The fuming lieutenant punched in the number without a thought, unaware Anna danced on his head, causing him to shake. No flies in this room; only Anna pricking his damn conscience.

"Stop calling me at this number. How many times do I have to tell you?" Reynolds' soft voice carried a malevolent warning.

Anna knew and hated the voice on the other end. Small world indeed.

Cummings carried on relentlessly, ignoring the threat in the words. "Reynolds, your lieutenant is a problem. She's sticking her nose in shit best left alone."

The frazzled policeman pushed his hands through his thinning hair as Anna imitated her best line dance with a few improvisational moves thrown in to keep him scratching.

"When you called the first time, I told you Goldberg should'a been a tracker or an African wild dog. Once she gets a whiff of a scent, she won't let go." Reynolds' voice dropped an octave. Since earning a graduate degree at MSU, the chief's screw-up of the Dowling murder created an opening for him to become Battle Creek's first black chief of police. Cummings was not going to ruin this for him. With McConnell opting for early retirement and the black community demanding changes, Reynolds' rose to the top of the search committee's list of candidates. Under his interim leadership, the Cold Case Team was proactive and productive. If the interim leader played his cards right, and Goldberg brought in Hoskins, he'd be the next chief.

Jerald Dowling had taken the plea deal. The difference between natural life and the possibility of parole after twenty-five years convinced him to go away quietly. High placed people in the community started deserting the business man in favor of Amie Rivers. As executor of her sister's estate and the family trust, Rivers informed the City Manager she was in contact with an Indiana based company who's empty plant, trained workers, and incentives made a move from Battle Creek to Fort Wayne, Indiana worthwhile. Economics versus friendship. Economics won!

"If she keeps messing with me, she'll end up in a boxcar." Cummings aimed his gun and shot at a target practice body on the wall. Click! The chamber was empty. Cummings leaned forward, breathing until he was in control again.

"Stop freaking out. I told you about shitting in your backyard. That's why you hightailed it out of here in the first place." Reynolds reminded Cummings.

"The first one was an accident." Cummings' eyes rolled around. His palms grew sweaty. "She was required to give me the same respect she gave her damn pimp. He made her turn out the twelve and thirteen-year-olds in the neighborhood, then beat her ass every day. I needed the collar, and she wouldn't roll on him."

As rookies, Reynolds and Cummings were assigned to the BCPD vice squad. Their job was to enforce laws against drug dealers and street-level prostitution. Don't mess with the johns. Focus on busting the women and racking up fines until the working girls developed a rap sheet and could be arrested.

Open air solicitation going on around homes, alleys, parking in lots behind a prominent church and an elementary school. The perpetrators were dumping used condoms in the parking lots. Filth. Fed up with the police and their unwillingness to be vigilant with the johns, a local women's group engaged in some undercover snooping, took pictures of the johns' license plates and of men soliciting the women.

The community women marched on City Hall, politicizing the agenda of arresting girls and women while letting the married, clergy, local businessmen go free. They showed pictures of the two rookie cops arresting the women: the women smiling on the way out of jail and documenting the same women back on the streets within hours.

The turning point came when a local pimp turned out thirteen- and fourteen-year-old girls. Multiple officers also accepted bribes from pimps to ignore individual girls and boys. The cops would

send the kids home with stern warnings. The next day their pimp would move them to another area and start over again. The City Commission turned up the heat to clean up the area and dismantle the prostitution ring. Cummings buckled under the pressure. Vicious beatings of women were covered up by other officers. Pimps were shaken down.

"So, you killed a girl." Reynolds mistaken allegiance to his former partner could still reach out and ruin his career.

"And you helped me cover it up." Cummings' heart rate accelerated, and his pupils dilated. "So easy. These bitches ain't worth shit. The damn pimp put another girl out there trafficking little kids the next week after she disappeared."

Reynolds cleaned up Cummings messes as dictated by The Blue Line.

Women's groups demanded drug treatment and rehabilitation services for the women, many of whom suffered from addiction and homelessness. These proposed services would cut into the police department's budget, lessening the number of officers on the streets. The commissioners didn't take the women seriously until one of them ran for the City Commission and won. The newly elected commissioner used her community platform to call attention to the disparate treatment of women versus the men who patronized them.

"Cummings don't call me again! You got options. You can shut her down by catching this perp, or she can have an accident. I don't care which option you choose."

Goldberg, this some deep shit. You better have some reasoning skills because I got a feelin' these boys would trade you for Sugar Man. Thank God, you got me looking out for' you.

CHAPTER TWENTY-EIGHT

"Lt. Goldberg, this is Landon Miller. Hoskins is at the homeless camp behind the Amtrak Station. I just saw him, plain as day. He didn't see me, though." After the beating, Sugar Man moved on to another camp. Landon had lost the man's trail temporarily, but painstakingly went to every hole where homeless camps existed along I-94 until he'd tracked the killer down.

"Didn't I tell you to let me do this by the book?" Goldberg understood where Anna's spirit got her stubbornness. Her friends and family trampled on this investigation at every turn.

Landon snorted, "You need to get rid of yo snitch, Amal. He gave Hoskins up with the right pressure."

"Mr. Miller, go back to building houses and leave police matters to the professionals."

"Then get off your asses and arrest him." Miller hung up.

Landon saw more in me than I saw in myself. I was too stubborn to let my mistakes with Keenan go. Dug in my heels to prove what point. I picked a murdering thug when a good man was right there for me. Too late... Landon embodied all the character traits she wanted in a mate.

No, he didn't wear $1,200 suits or drive anything except work trucks. Her forever friend owned a profitable business, saved, and invested his money. He loved Turquoise and had wanted to give her a full-time father living under the same roof as her mother.

* * *

"We missed him," muttered Officer McGill, evading her eyes. At five-foot-nine the youthful officer could have been playing linebacker for Western Michigan University's Broncos football team instead of being nonchalant about this job. He faced Goldberg and Cummings and gave the report. "We got over here as soon as you gave the order. We've been interviewing informants, everyone we can talk to, and showing his picture around."

Ten minutes after Goldberg called in the location, unmarked cars, undercover cops, and on-duty officers converged on the McDonalds located on Kalamazoo Street, a place where the homeless ate and used the facilities. The officers fanned out in all directions, looking for the murderer. Situated on a busy downtown street near the Amtrak and bus stations, homeless men and women loitered around the fast-food restaurant, careful to observe the thirty-minute time limit. Several men fit the general description Fawn gave the police.

"What did you learn?" Cummings asked. Like Goldberg, he was being harassed and threatened by his superiors who wanted Hoskins off the street before another woman was murdered. Today's *Gazette* newspaper editorial chastised the police department and Cummings by name for not cleaning up the area, and for permitting the homeless, streetwalkers, and others to loiter downtown. The Gazette's wealthy owner's influence extended beyond the 80,000 residents of the town. Kalamazoo's reputation as an All-American city was up for grabs unless the department performed their job and rid the city of criminal elements.

"Hoskins mainly keeps to himself, doesn't say much. Nobody knows where he sleeps. We went to the mission and showed his picture. They remember him eating in the dining area and taking a shower a couple of times. He wasn't allowed to stay overnight because he didn't have any identification."

Why didn't they call the tip line if they thought it was him? No wonder people go missing. Not my monkey...not my show.

"How come your people didn't tell us this before?" Goldberg wanted to tackle this fresh-faced cop. Take him down by grabbing his knees and wrestling him to the ground, pummeling him until he learned to be more diligent in catching a murder suspect.

McGill dropped his head, mumbling. "Too much going on. It got overlooked, Lieutenant."

What's the point of a Joint Task Force if everybody still wants to be the Lone Ranger? Cops should be forced to live on the street for a while. They might feel a little more compassion for the people they purported to protect and serve. Goldberg, he can't go far. All you came to do was catch one murderer. Instead, you're over here digging in stuff that ain't none of your bizness. Just help me take down Sugar Man and then you can do whatever.

Goldberg had lost her objectivity. Her attempts at shutting out Anna weren't working as the ghost gained strength. Anna knew they were close to catching Hoskins and the troubled spirit was determined to take him down alive. "Give it a rest, Anna. We're close to wrapping this up, and I gotta keep my wits about me. Keep the main thing the main thing. Capturing Willie Earl Hoskins. Preventing the murder of another woman."

"When Hoskins showed up, he befriended the old-timer sitting over there." McGill pointed to a rail-thin white man with a dirty gray beard covering much of his face, his thin hair covered with a stocking cap. The man's gnarly fingers wrapped around a Big Mac as though he didn't have a care in the world.

"We kept the old timer here, thinking he might be useful." The youthful cop was attempting to make-up for his earlier lapse in judgment.

Sylvia introduced herself to the old man and showed him Hoskins' photo.

The old timer mumbled, "He asked a lot of questions about the mission. Whether they could give him a train ticket to get out of here."

Who knew cops spent so much time on bullshit while Willie Earl's having sex, then killing and robbing women?

Officer McGill's partner reported in, his low-pitched voice scared. "While we were fanning around the area, Hoskins was sighted sitting over there in the corner. He must have picked up our scent and snuck past our decoys."

McGill shrunk in stature, unable to meet Goldberg's intense stare. "He left his jacket and hat behind, put his head down and walked out the back way. Either he's on the hunt, or he's already picked another victim."

"How long has he been gone?" Goldberg checked her watch.

"Ten minutes, max."

Cummings gritted his teeth, punched the air. "Too long. Let's get moving."

CHAPTER TWENTY-NINE

"Have you seen this man?" Hoskins snarled. Damn wanted posters plastered with his mugshot. On trees, light poles, the library. The mission. McDonald's. All around the place. Lying about him on television and the radio. If he made a mistake now, the police might find him before he could replace what he'd lost when them bastards raided the homeless camp. He had to get out of this damn area.

Anna was a ball of pure wrath. Sugar Man was dragging another woman to the railroad yard. She felt the fury that ran red through his brain. He was trapped. With all the signs of his face around town, television screens blasting his picture and the reward money. She had to get Goldberg. Even she could only be in one place a time. If she stayed here, he might kill and get away again.

Hoskins opened the boxcar door, fleetingly scanned the interior, and pushed the prostitute into the dark car that smelled of straw and manure. The woman smiled through her rotted teeth and alcohol-induced fog. He pushed her to her knees.

"Where's my money?" Her words were clear enough, her back straight.

Hoskins showed her a wad of bills, stuffed them back in his sweatpants pocket. "You'll get yours. Now get to work." A malevolent grin spread across his face as he pushed down his clothing and pulled out his rod.

She found the right pressure spot and suctioned him into her mouth like a pro.

Acting like them other bitches, thinking she was doing something no one else could do. About five minutes later, Hoskins shot his load all over her face and chest, pushing her away.

She opened her mouth and hand simultaneously to demand her money. Hoskins slammed his fist into her face, knocking her to the floor. Then he grabbed her by her wrists, jerking her up, the force breaking her left wrist. Her pain-filled screams sent chills through him as he tried to shut her up, knocking her back on the straw and debris-strewn floor.

Anna spotted the box cutter and guided the young woman's right hand to the sharp object. The prostitute closed her fingers around the cutter. "Fuck you!" she bellowed, slicing her fingers on the box cutter buried in the pile of crap.

Hoskins leaned in to punch her again. She raised her hand and slashed his face down the left side, close to the eye and down his cheek, reopening the wound and cutting to the bone.

"Bitch!" Blood spurted, blurring his vision. The blistering pain jolted him back a few feet, stumbling, giving her room to make a run for the door. Her ear-piercing screams calling out to God's angels to rescue her from the madman intent on obliterating her from the face of the earth.

Hoskins' meaty fist lunged for the prostitute. She slashed his hand. He grunted, pain radiating from his hand as well as his face.

Slick warm blood covered him, impeding his forward progress. The pain disoriented him, making his movements slower.

Anna's energy pulsed between the two combatants, forcing Sugar Man back a couple of feet. He was raging, beyond caring. All humanity had been beaten out of him. He grabbed the girl's broken wrist, shaking her. Whenever he yanked her close to him, Anna's frenetic energy pushed the girl to strike his hands and chest, gouging skin, inflicting pain.

Hoskins growled like a dying pig and let go of the young prostitute's wrist. His knees caved in beneath him. No woman had ever hit him back. He felt like a bitch again, helpless, abused. He shook his head, snarling at his prey.

The woman scrambled away, screaming, getting closer to the door. As she pushed the handle of the boxcar, Hoskins grabbed her from behind, knocking her to the floor.

Anna kicked up the straw into his face, blinding him and stopping him from stomping the woman to death. You're not killing another woman. You are goin down, and I'm the one who's gonna take you out. His nemesis' energy force struck him in his crotch, forcing a high-pitched girly scream as he grabbed his jewels.

CHAPTER THIRTY

G oldberg heard the screaming as she sprinted toward the boxcar, ahead of Cummings and the rest of the team. She pushed against the partially-open door. "POLICE!!!"

Alive, Goldberg! Alive!! Anna fought too many obstacles to confront Sugar Man for Goldberg to kill him. Her thirst for vengeance was not to see him in hell yet. Sugar Man had to go back in jail. Only this time, he would be unable to defend himself, and no one would come to his rescue, either financially or emotionally. Being at the mercy of his cellmate would provide the vengeance she needed and allow her spirit to catch up with her body.

Hoskins' was disoriented, holding his crotch with one hand and his other bloody fist raised. "I'm not goin back to prison. You gonna get this woman killed if you don't close that door and hightail it out of here. I'm almost done with her."

The intended murder victim lunged at him, waving the dripping box cutter wildly, slicing his shoulder. No man would ever use her again and rob her of her pay. She'd left her pimp in Detroit with visible scars. That man would think several times before coming at any woman with a gun.

"Police!" Goldberg's service revolver was drawn. "Hoskins, back away from the woman before I shoot yo ass!"

Anna slammed her elbow into his chest.

Willie Earl battled the second opponent who was hitting his chest and kicking his legs as well as the younger woman weaving in front of him. He screamed hysterically, "Stop it, Anna. You are dead. I know you dead." Hoskins struggled to stand upright.

Goldberg steadied her gun to take Hoskins out before he did any more damage. Regardless of Anna's desires, this sick puppy was going to be put down. He could live another fifty years on the State's dole if she didn't kill him now.

"Don't shoot to kill!" Anna hissed at Goldberg. "He ain't getting away easy. My family's been through too much not to have a chance to see him at trial. Maybe he'll tell them why he killed me and then they can move on."

Goldberg lowered the shot from Hoskins' head to his back and fired one shot in his right ass cheek. Hoskins yelped, but he didn't move away from the prostitute who was still stabbing blindly at the air. This woman could give lessons to the domestic violence victims Goldberg worked with.

Anna's life-force jumped and pushed Goldberg's hand. Goldberg got off two shots, one finding an entry at the base of the convict's spine.

Hoskins' high-pitched scream filled the boxcar as his legs no longer held him up and he fell to the floor.

Anna's shove propelled Goldberg on top of Hoskins; her life force pummeling Hoskins' head with the butt of the gun. Blood and gore streamed down into his eyes. He howled like a dog with his foot clamped in a trap set for a bear. The weapon connected with a thud against his skull and knocked him over on his side. I hope the bullets fragments must be pulled out one at the time. Let the suffering begin right now.

Goldberg didn't try to stop Anna from having her way with Hoskins. He'd killed numerous women for the few dollars they earned on the street, then tossed them aside like trash. Their loved ones probably worried when they didn't show up and now would look up to see two uniformed officers informing them of the gruesome details of their death.

The prostitute crawled away from Hoskins but not before connecting with one more cut to his head. Pain shot through her broken left wrist. She moaned. Her right wrist stung from the cuts, and tears ran down her face as she inched away, knowing the cops didn't give a damn about her welfare. They got the guy they came for, and now she was a nuisance.

"Knock his ass out!" Anna wouldn't be vindicated until Sugar Man was immobilized, in cuffs and headed back to Ionia. Forget the trial. There were enough bodies to make that outcome a reality. When Sugar Man's fantasy plans for getting his old drug life back evaporated, he took the bitterness out on her. After getting a taste of the blood rush, he'd picked women randomly. He wasn't trying to go straight.

Cummings and his team heard Hoskins screams as they sprinted into the boxcar with guns drawn, rushing into the melee. Goldberg shouted "Stop!" as she shook the fiery haze from her brain, reeling from the stench of perspiration-soaked clothing, sex, and vomit. Other cops rushed to the scene, one group intent on putting shackles on Hoskins' hands.

Hoskins terrified screams didn't deter the officers. "My legs.... can't feel my legs."

Goldberg hollered, "Don't touch him! He's got a bullet in his spine!" If not for Anna, he'd be waiting for a body bag instead of an emergency vehicle to take him to the nearest emergency room. "Mirandize him before he passes out."

Cummings barked, "Call for two buses and the sweepers." He shook his head at Goldberg. What cop with half a brain left rubbish like that alive for the State to house and feed for the rest of his life? Damn. Not only did Goldberg get here first, but she'd also immobilized the killer and was taking him in alive. She'd get a commendation and probably a promotion for solving five murders in his town. After he mirandized the screaming bitch, Cummings hissed, "Goldberg, you're leaving us with the mess of paperwork… and a trial. Why didn't you kill the s.o.b? You had a clear shot." He spat. "Women."

When the prison doors close this time, it's forever. I'm waiting for that. No more women to prey on. Time to remember how he was brought down by the woman whose lifeless body he spat on. She'd remind him for the rest of his life.

Goldberg ignored Cummings. How do you say I'm led around by a freaking ghost who wants vengeance? The only way to get her out of my life was to give her what she wanted. I want my damn life back more than I want another kill on my record.

Goldberg left Hoskins' bloody, bulleted body to Cummings. Kneeling beside the bleeding streetwalker, Goldberg wrested the box cutter from the victim's hand. The caring woman's advocate assessed the damage done by Hoskins's beating. As the adrenaline rush left the woman-child, she slumped to the filthy floor. Her breathing was shallow, and she was going into shock.

Goldberg whispered in her ear. "You're a fighter, a survivor. You took him down. We owe you." Goldberg didn't dare touch the broken wrist. Without a stent, she would only inflict more pain. Where was the damn bus?

Anna screamed at the survivor, blasting Goldberg's senses. "Don't faint! I know you hurt bad, but you fought back!"

CHAPTER THIRTY-ONE

*S*ugar Man's in custody, disabled and at the mercy of others. He won't harm another woman in this lifetime. Keep him always shackled to the hospital bed. Make him beg for a drink of water or a bite of food. But at least he's alive to suffer.

Desiring a closer look, Anna balanced on Sugar Man's battered shoulder as Bronson Methodist Hospital's elite neurological and trauma surgical team prepped him for surgery. The God of Morpheus temporarily alleviated his pain. When the result of the operation is disclosed, he'll wish he'd never heard my name, but he won't forget me. Ever. Especially when he's sent back to Ionia and needing help with the most basic human functioning.

Dr. James, neurosurgeon and Dr. McGee, trauma surgeon pored over the x-rays, determining their surgery strategy. Dr. James pinpointed the damage to the spinal cord. "One bullet severed the spinal cord at T-10. The trauma team's been poking him with no response since we put him on the table. There was immediate paralysis of his legs. We can't undo the paralysis to his legs. We need to clean up the area, remove the bullets and bone, and stop the leakage of spinal fluid. We can stabilize the spine with screws."

For twenty years, James had operated on guys like this. It never got easier. As his skills increased, so did the severity of cases he was called in to operate on: victims of gang fights, drug busts, and cops shooting gangsters during the commission of a felony. When he had free time, the neurosurgeon lectured to both community leaders and young people about gun violence and its lasting negative impact. Nothing romanticized like Wesley Snipes in the Sugar Hill movie. For those who didn't die, they lived with paralyzed limbs and chronic diseases. They were dependent on caregivers for the gazillion tasks the ordinary person takes for granted. Imagine a fly buzzing around your nose and being unable to swat it away.

Anna pulsed between James and McGee as they discussed options to save Sugar Man's life. Corrections is getting ready to spend a grip on surgery for this scum bucket! But no pity party or bleeding-heart doctors' gon' stop him from spending the rest of his natural life in jail. Who makes these damn rules?

"After we stabilize the spine, there are bullet fragments to get out, especially in his lungs and liver to ensure he's not bleeding into the chest." Dr. McGee's jaw tightened as he checked the x-rays one final time. "We're going to need a vascular surgeon to address the blood loss and determine if the abdominal aorta was nicked after the bullets ricocheted.

James sent a text to his chief resident to call for a vascular surgeon. She relayed that one would be available.

McGee grumbled. "James, do you ever ask yourself why we patch these guys up after they push drugs, kill numerous people, and tear up our community?"

James shook his head negatively. "I took an oath to heal people. Let's get scrubbed. He's ready. As soon as the vascular guy gets in

here, we've got a good seven hours of work ahead of us. After that, the second surgery team goes in to clean up the internal injuries."

Twelve hours later, Hoskins was wheeled into ICU with an NG tube down his throat and morphine pumping through his veins. Attesting to his level of pre-op violence, the doctors left specific notes for the post-surgery crew on how to manage the patient. Two armed guards took up their position outside his room.

Anna perched at the head of the bed, checking out the monitors. My work won't be done until he's wheeled up to the Ionia Prison cell door and is reunited with his boo.

CHAPTER THIRTY-TWO

"*G*oldberg, you my shero. You coulda killed Sugar Man. He's alive, and he's bout to get what he deserves.*"

"Barely alive and only because you moved my hand, Anna." Goldberg was an expert shot. She didn't leave garbage behind for the system to clean up. In addition to the paperwork and debriefings with Internal Affairs, she'd squared off with Reynolds. Politics! He'd ripped her a new one for not killing Hoskins. He knew her marksmanship skill levels and the details of her previous take downs.

One more nail in her coffin. Forget the collar. She defended her live takedown of Hoskins. Cummings sulked in the corner of the room. Two women, one of them a prostitute, and the other an overzealous cop he'd hated on sight, took down a crazed two hundred plus pound murderer. When the full story got around the station, Cummings was going to have to bust a few heads or endure months of sniggers and bad jokes.

In the early morning hours, Goldberg and Cummings staggered into Tasha Murphy's hospital room, bleary from lack of sleep, and battered from meeting with their superiors. Tasha was groggy after

the surgery to set the delicate bones of her left wrist. She had a black eye, a chipped front tooth, and a bruised face. Her four cracked ribs were bound, and she'd been given a high dose of painkillers.

"Tasha, I'm Lieutenant Goldberg, and this is Captain Cummings." Cummings barely eyeballed the battered woman.

Tasha blinked several times as if forcing her brain and eyes to coordinate. She was in constant pain, and the doctors weren't forthcoming about the extent of her injuries or prognosis.

"We won't stay long, but we need your help." After waiting for the tiny nod, Goldberg asked the battered young woman "Tell us what happened."

What's up with you people? The girl has been sexually assaulted, beaten down, nearly killed. Look at the black circles around her eyes. Scratches and bruises. Can't you wait until later today, let her get some sleep? Sugar Man ain't going nowhere. He's in ICU, and the doctors say it'll be at least twenty-four hours before he regains consciousness. He's gonna be here a couple of weeks to a month. Then he goes to rehab.

He's never goin to walk again. That much is clear. I'm pleading with God that he spends the rest of his miserable days in a tiny cell where someone must haul his ass into the top bunk, hand him a stankin' urinal to piss in. Forget about taking a shower. Hose him down when he too putrid to be around other people. I'm beggin God that he sees my face whenever he begs for help.

"Later Anna. I've got work to do here. It's no longer about you." Without Anna's intervention, Tasha would be another statistic. She'd found Tasha's wallet in the zippered inside pocket of her threadbare jacket.

Anna's help was no longer required. Goldberg had to clean up the loose ends and prepare this case for trial. Because Hoskins was on parole when he killed Anna, he was headed back to prison. Then

there were the other women who'd been murdered while Hoskins was evading law enforcement. Two counties. Two different jurisdictions.

Goldberg's dogged intruder needed to relax and let her soul reunite with her body. It was essential Goldberg get the hell out of Kalamazoo before Cummings could plot his revenge against her. She'd gotten too close to his dirty practices, and Cummings was in cover-up mode up to his glacial blue eyes.

Tasha's dry lips barely parted. Goldberg picked up the glass of ice chips on the hospital stand, and gently placed the ice chips to the young girl's lips. Moving a couple of chips with her tongue, Tasha moistened her lips. Goldberg wiped her mouth with the moistened towelette on the hospital stand. She looked around, saw a chair, pulled it closer and sat, feeding Tasha more ice chips.

"I was walking to the boarding house… coming back from the Mission where I'd just applied for some financial help. This john comes along." Tasha's slurred speech was hesitant. "He offered me $50 for a blow job. I was down to my last five dollars." She whooshed out air. "This was not the worst beating I ever took."

Stupid women. "Didn't you see the wanted posters out there?" Cummings shot her a hateful glance.

Goldberg patted the girl's hand. No Quantico training about victimology would ever reconcile with how women survived on the street.

"Yeah. I didn't really look at his face." Tasha pushed the pain pump.

Goldberg had five minutes max before the morphine kicked in.

Tasha shook her head from side to side on the pillow. "New to town. Smaller town, fewer hassles than Detroit. Couple women told me … where the safe houses are. I'm renting a cheap room. My plan…turn a few tricks, get a stake. Find a real job… Start living."

She rushed the words as if trying to tell the story before the meds coursing through her system shut out the pain.

All the advertising they'd done, and Hoskins still slipped through the cracks. Without Landon's tip, Goldberg would be examining another dead body.

Cummings grumbled an aside to Goldberg. "Stupid heifer should'a kept her ass in Detroit. We got enough rubbish on the streets already."

"We're investigating a crime, Lieutenant. Not moralizing." Goldberg shot him a side-eye.

Cummings dropped his eyes first. This was effed up. Upstaged by two women. He could kiss any upward mobility goodbye. He'd been invincible. No one connected the dots before. He'd have to figure out a way to make the evidence she'd uncovered disappear. And he couldn't retaliate directly against Goldberg because she was worse than any foe he'd ever dealt with.

Goldberg resumed the interrogation. "Where'd you learn to fight? You messed his face up. He's got enough stitches he could pass for a relative of Frankenstein." Goldberg patted Tasha's hand. Goldberg promised the doctor she wouldn't overtax Tasha. The cop fed her more ice chips.

Tasha's laugh was hollow and pained-filled. "I was on the streets… at thirteen. My mama, my sisters…all on the stroll … keep it in the family. I w-w-wanted to be a dancer… k-kick, flip, mix it up with the best dancers… came in handy." She closed her eyes, shuddered. Turning tricks, avoiding pimps who'd take her money and beat her into submission. She wasn't like her mother and sisters who stayed hopped up on drugs. After making the decision to leave Detroit, she wasn't going back. Today was a reminder of that old life. She came here for a new start, and if that included a women's shelter until she got a job, so be it. She wasn't built for degradation and beatings.

Goldberg mused her strength and flexibility probably saved her life. "How old are you?"

"Eighteen." She looked Goldberg in the eye, ignoring Cummings. "He knocked me back on the floor, and my hand fell on the box cutter."

When you hear somebody say fight like a girl, they ain't playing. Tasha beat the hell out of him. She knew what I didn't. Sugar Man was all about his survival. She did what I couldn't. He knocked her down. She didn't curl up in a ball and let him pound her body. Yeah, I helped with the box-cutter, but it was all her. Tasha's will to survive was stronger than mine.

Tasha held up her bandaged hand. Her eyes were starting to droop, her body relaxing, succumbing to the powerful drugs coursing through her body. "I'm not able to do much… both hands bandaged…I can't work. I'll figure it out." She closed her eyes and snorted softly.

Told you to wait, Goldberg, until the girl's in better shape. Be relieved she had more sense than me. She fought back. She kicked his sorry ass.

Don't worry, Anna. We're going to help her get on her feet and out of the life. She would help this girl obtain a decent job and a support network…maybe Tasha could use her experience to help other women. A survivor's message was better than the cops any day of the week.

CHAPTER THIRTY-THREE

Suing First Lady Watson was as close as Lee Roy Scott came to acknowledging his yearning for revenge. First Lady had blood on her hands. Lenore Watson created and shaped the prison ministry and knew her brother was the leader in the demonic shit resulting in Anna's death.

The Scott family's repeated accusations and the Safe and Just Michigan agency inquiry turned up additional incriminating information that linked the Prison Ministry's activities to Brady Johnson, Lenore Watson, and Liberty International Church. When the graphic details hit social media, the church, already crippled spiritually and financially not desiring more scandal, encouraged the church's liability insurance company to pay off Lee Roy Scott.

Vindication for my family. Folks saying Lee Roy Scott responsible for splitting the church. He's looking out for my good name and Turquoise. She can't go around with her head down because of what I did.

Lee Roy, Kerri, and Melany sat with their lawyer at one end of the board table at Liberty Nondenominational Church while Pastor, First Lady, the few remaining deacons, counsel, and the church's liability insurance company sat at the other end.

Lee Roy jumped in before the others could read the summary. "Brady Johnson controlled the drugs and money smuggled in through items the women donated to the prison in the name of the Liberty Nondenominational Church Prison Ministry. I been telling y'all that since Anna's death."

"There are lots of issues at Ionia. Overcrowding is a big issue. Three-strike laws are turning people into habitual criminals. Locking guys up for distribution of drugs and watching them turn into animals. The State sent in new officers to replace some fired guards. The fired officers were low men on the totem pole, low pay, and the worst jobs. By keeping their eyes open, they quickly learned Brady Johnson was a dangerous man. He was also cunning and had help from the outside. It was widely acknowledged that Johnson was laying low until the official investigation involving the Prison Ministry was concluded.

Joye Nelson also investigated discreetly. She fed the information to the right people who knew how to get to the bottom of this mess. First Lady Watson had operated her ministry in one form or another for ten or so years.

The lawyer picked up his report again. "There's a no contact order between First Lady and her brother so that they can't coordinate their testimony. The auditors have been able to glean some information from the First Lady's computer, including where and from whom she purchased most of the items the women delivered to the prison."

Pastor Watson kept his eyes downcast. He'd been duped by his wife. A woman like her wouldn't do well in prison. But once she broke down and confessed, he told her if she cooperated, it would be easier for her. She brushed him off.

"Johnson had a lucrative sideline dealing in contraband, mostly doctored cigarettes and toiletries. He paid off the guy who ran the various ministries inside the prison and made sure no one snitched. He was also able to smuggle items out of the prison using the ministry."

"I tole y'all it was a front for bringing in drugs, money, and goods."

"To let you know the level of cunning that went into the scheme, the prison psychologist evaluated Hoskins when he arrived. The doctor wrote that Hoskins was at high risk for sexual victimization. Yet, Hoskins ended up sharing a cell with Johnson, a serial sex offender serving twenty-five years to life for murder."

At the end of the meeting, Lee Roy demanded a public apology from the pulpit in addition to the money. No amount of money would bring back Anna or restore Turquoise's life to what it was before her mother was murdered. But the church members and the town needed to know Anna was not some loose woman. She'd been led astray within the church whose job it was to lift her up and encourage her. He wouldn't sign the settlement until he received his public apology.

The next Sunday, with the media in attendance to write the epitaph, Pastor Watson resigned his position as senior pastor. "My wife and I are stepping away from ministry to fix our marital problems. What happened here on our watch resulted in the death of a woman who thought she was following God's plan as laid out by her church leaders. Weasel words like I'm sorry and we didn't know won't erase the damaging consequences to Anna Marie Scott, Turquoise, or the Scott family. The whispers in the community won't end until we accept full responsibility for our actions and begin to atone for the mess we created."

Pastor Watson wiped his wet brow and held out his hands beseechingly, "Believe me, God is dealing with us individually and as a couple. No other church is willing to accept our leadership currently. And the truth is, we don't deserve to be in those roles. Until God is pleased with our restitution and sincere changes, we'll pray for His grace and mercy toward us. We will find secular employment to pay our share of the fine to the Scotts. This settlement is a combined repayment plan from the insurance company and from our assets. The courts will monitor the repayment plan. In the event we don't comply, the state has attached our pensions and other assets. Money alone won't undo the harm we caused. My wife simply asks that you keep us lifted before God as we seek to atone for the harm and dissention we caused."

Pastor Watson's resignation was immediate. He left town with his disgraced wife. Rumors swirled around the congregation about the details of the settlement, but the Scotts remained close mouthed. The family withdrew from church life and eventually found another place to worship. The sanctuary and its people were too visible reminders of Anna.

Out of the need for atonement, Liberty International's newly appointed minister met with Lee Roy and his brothers. The pastor offered his condolences, ensured the payments would arrive on time, and finally outlined their revised outreach ministry. The prison ministry would be headed up by the male leaders, not single women. The new pastor reminded the congregation that when the early church was formed, Paul and Silas walked through the prisons. The plan was not to exclude women but for the brethren to be the messengers of Christ, bringing liberation to the captives. There were legitimate roles for women but being tempted or put in danger didn't square up with his version of service to God.

Now that's what I'm talking about. I had a strong foundation and threw it all away. Misguided…like the song says…looking for love in all the wrong places. Stubborn like my daddy. The hole in his heart won't go away, but maybe he can sleep better now. I sing my mama's favorite hymns sometime so he can settle in and rest. One day, he'll sleep more than a few hours.

CHAPTER THIRTY-FOUR

In the nine months leading up to the trial, the newspapers and other media outlets shared every gruesome detail of Willie Earl Hoskins' crime spree. Hoskins was transported to the Calhoun County jail following a two-month stay in rehab to reestablish a minor level of mobility. Beyond the basics, none of the hospital's therapists were willing to work with Hoskins, saying he was strong as a bull, a menace, and they feared for their safety. The therapists knew of his crimes. His torso and upper body strength were turn offs. The presence of two armed guards did not change their willingness to render aid.

Seventy-year-old Judge Delaney presided over the Calhoun County trial. when first elected to the bench, he was a zealous young prosecutor. His judicial philosophy stemmed from Richard Nixon's law and order campaign, mandatory sentences, and three strikes law. Right off the bat, Judge Delany denied the Public Defender's appeals for a specialized wheelchair for Hoskins and other accommodations for his disability.

The judge lectured both lawyers, "This trial is a formality. Hoskins was out on parole and killed a woman before he'd been on the streets

for one day. If it were up to me, he'd have been back at Ionia when the physicians declared he was ready for physical rehabilitation. We invest money in the prison system to deal with these matters."

Yea, Judge. I know I'm in the best hands with you. He's not gonna be able to play on anybody's sympathy and get sent to some cushy facility where he can bully other people. He's going down.

The public defender, Desmond Taylor, fresh from passing the Michigan Bar, and the newest member of the Public Defender's office was assigned to defend Hoskins. Hoskins was only his second case. Nothing could change the outcome, but his supervisor told him to put forth a credible defense regardless of the circumstances because "that's what we do."

Public Defender Taylor and Hoskins, wearing an orange jumpsuit, sat at the defense table. Hoskins perched on a customized foam cushion and was strapped to the chair, his useless legs twitching and spasming. His gaunt face, scarred from the fight with the young prostitute, needed a shave. Even though his legs no longer functioned, hours of physical therapy increased Hoskins upper body strength. He radiated pure hatred. Armed security guards stood at the ready.

Anna perched on his shoulder and watched him twitch. Where yo boys at now, Sugar Man? Nobody wants to be associated with you. You are a loser, can't walk, gotta take a piss in a jar. Gotta have help in and out of bed. Man, I might be dead, but you gonna remember me with ev'ry breath you take.

The prisoner twitched until his lawyer leaned over and asked, "what's wrong?"

"She... Anna .... I can feel her."

"What is wrong with you? There's no one at this table except you and me. The judge is watching you. You need to calm down."

"Anna. I told you. She was there when that bitch tried to kill me. Anna helped her try to kill me. There's no way that girl could hurt me lak that on her own."

There was nothing in the law books about this level of insanity. Voices. Dead people. Hallucinations. "Hoskins, if you don't cut out the crazy talk, you're going to end up in the psych ward which is worse than the general population."

Ha! Told you it was just you and me from here on out. Nobody believes you.

The prosecutor, Judson Harmon, blistering opening statement set the tone for the trial and how he intended to manage the District Attorney's office should he win. As he described the heinous crime scene and showed the graphic pictures to the jury, one juror slumped to the floor.

The Scott family and their supporters, seated behind the prosecutor, huddled together, and wept. *Daddy, I'm so sorry.*

Judge Delaney called a brief recess to attend to the juror and allow the Scott family time to regain some calm.

Having gotten the jury on his side with the forensic information and the gruesome autopsy photographs, the prosecutor paraded out Lieutenants Sylvia Goldberg and Brian Cummings as the state's star witnesses. Harmon guided them through carefully orchestrated testimonies detailing the actions of Willie Earl Hoskins, his crimes in Kalamazoo, and their takedown of Hoskins in the box car. Knowing what was at stake, the two investigators stuck to the facts of the investigation at hand, including the anonymous tips that alerted them to Hoskins' whereabouts.

The prosecutor subpoenaed Hoskins' posse: Amal and Louie. The litigator declared the two men hostile witnesses and forced them to recount the activities of that early Thursday morning, finally forcing

them to admit on record Hoskins was in a rage before dropping him off at Anna Marie Scott's house. Amal squirmed in the seat and tried to minimize his role in what went down. The Battle Creek police had cut him loose as an informant. On his own without their protection, the weasel's days were numbered unless he could get out of town as soon as this trial was concluded.

Louie, serving time at Jackson State Penitentiary for accessory to murder and various unrelated drug offenses, was contemptuous when he was asked to describe what "putting a bitch in her place" meant. He sneered at the Scott family huddled together in pain, surrounded by their friends and community members as he revealed in excruciating detail how Hoskins drank a fifth of cognac, smoked blunts, and recounted his grievances against Anna Marie and all the women who did him wrong.

Hoskins was petrified of confronting The Godfather who'd lied to him and stole his business, but the convicted criminal would show he was a man when he beat that bitch down. The jury looked from Louie to Hoskins, his fate sealed by the malevolent looks they cast toward him.

When Taylor stood to present his opening arguments, Harmon doodled on his yellow notepad, interrupted Taylor, and with switchblade precision, ripped apart every petty point of the pro forma bullshit. The Public Defender was supposed to get Hoskins to plead out and save the taxpayers the cost of this trial. Still, the green public defender was boosting Harmon's pre-election campaign for Attorney General.

The public defender had been unable to shake the testimony of the prosecution witnesses or dent the evidence against his client. He put forward three witnesses for the defense. Dr. James was compelled to testify to the condition of the accused, including the

physical trauma he sustained and the ongoing need for a clean and sanitary environment.

An officer from Ionia testified Hoskins had been targeted by several gangs during his previous stay. He reported the unprovoked beatings as well as food and water deprivation. Hoskins had filed complaints against several officers on his way out of the facility. On his reentry, he'd be labeled a snitch. In his compromised physical condition, he was a bigger target for guards and inmates.

To convince the jury of his client's deteriorating condition, Taylor spent an entire day guiding the university professor who advocated for prison reform through the inadequacies of the state's facilities. The professor showed the actual conditions at Ionia, including the cell block, prison hospital, and rehabilitation facilities. Given the ratio of health care staff to inmates, the invalid might receive therapy once a week. Hoskins would decline rapidly without the intense therapy he required to maintain his current functioning. The professor concluded Hoskins should be assigned to a prison hospital where he could receive ongoing care.

The prosecutor demolished the witness by reminding him that Hoskins killed six women without remorse. His current injuries occurred during the rape and attempted murder of another woman. Why should the people have sympathy for him?

In his closing arguments, Taylor argued, "Ionia wasn't designed for disabled prisoners. My client is confined to a wheelchair. Mr. Hoskins has pins throughout his body. He won't be able to get needed physiotherapy. Based on previous interactions during his previous incarceration, the guards will not protect him. Show him mercy and allow him to serve his sentence at a prison hospital facility."

The jury deliberated for one hour and returned with the verdict: Guilty of first-degree murder with special circumstances. From

the bench, the judge pronounced the life sentence to the packed courtroom, "The defendant killed an additional five women in Kalamazoo. That's outside of my jurisdiction. Sentencing a man to six consecutive life sentences makes good copy, but natural life without parole is all he's got."

The judge concluded, "Willie Earl Hoskins uses a wheelchair for mobility, and he has numerous internal injuries that impact his daily functioning. He will live out his life in Ionia State Prison, a penitentiary designed to warehouse young men, not the aged or the infirm. May God have mercy on his soul."

EPILOGUE

Turquoise, it's time for me to go. You'll always feel my presence. Put your trust in God. He won't ever leave you. In Romans 8:38-39, Paul wrote, nothing can separate you or me from his love. I'm also leaving you a guardian. He's gonna be wherever you go until we're reunited. Look over there in the corner. He's wearing a blue soldier's uniform, letting you know he's a protector. His only job is to take care of you until we're reunited in the rapture. Can you see him?

Turquoise eyes flew to the corner, and she saw the shadowy outline of the blue uniform…her guardian. She nodded, tears clouding her vision. Her mommy never lied. Turquoise, with the loving guidance of her grandfather, had removed her bedroom furniture, clothing and a few keepsakes from the old house and now resided in Anna's former bedroom.

She was surrounded by grandpa, her aunts, Landon, and friends who'd help keep Anna's spirit alive. They promised to keep Turquoise safe. Anna would remain alive if they spoke her name, telling stories about her, reminding her only child that she'd once been here physically. Turquoise felt Anna's spirit and witnessed the power she had.

Don't tell anyone about the guardian. Some people can't deal with stuff they didn't experience themselves. They might not believe you.

"I love you, mommy."

Anna Scott flew out of the house, humming "Goin Up Yonder" as her soul floated around her family's home one last time. She flew past the new police station. Sylvia Goldberg was in Washington, DC. As soon as the trial ended, the lieutenant resigned and accepted a position at Quantico.

The stained living room carpet of her former home had been removed to reveal beautiful tiger pine hardwood floors. After Lee Roy and the family removed the pieces of furniture they wanted to keep, the remaining furniture had been sorted and staged to make the best impression for an estate sale. The bank had paid off the mortgage; Lee Roy could manage the taxes and utilities until the property sold.

Although the home's price was reduced twice, no buyer came forward. The realtor believed that because of the stability of the neighborhood, the house would eventually sell. It was a matter of time until the memories of the horrific murder receded.

"Give it time. The trial brought back the setting of the murder," The realtor told Lee Roy. The scene inside the house and the yellow tape outside the house had been splashed across the news media. The realtor invited members of her Native American tribe to sage the house, the ancient cleansing ritual used by Native American and shamanic cultures to remove negative energy from a space. They opened every window, walked through the house waving sticks of dried sage, and prayed for the evil spirits to depart forever. Afterward, they prayed over the house to return it to a sanctuary for a deserving family.

Anna's time was up. She was now ready to step out of this world. 2 Timothy 4:6-8 verbalized it best: the time of my departure is at hand.

Time to say goodbye, Daddy. So long, my sweet Turquoise. When you feel the breeze floating around you, it'll be me, flying away. I'm goin' up yonder to be with my Lord.

ANNA MARIE SCOTT placed her trust and future happiness in the hands of the wrong man. When she ends up dead, her restless soul is determined to bring her killer to justice. The local police are investigating her murder as typical domestic violence. Anna is earthbound until she finds a receptive soul to assist her.

Lt. Sylvia Goldberg, nearly burned-out head of the Domestic Violence Task Force, has few resources and even less respect from her fellow officers. However, Anna discovers a backdoor into Lt. Goldberg's empathetic powers and enlists her unwittingly to make solving her murder a priority.

Can Anna and Lt. Goldberg trample on enough police rules to capture her killer, thus paving the way for Anna to rest in peace finally?

www.ingramcontent.com/pod-product-compliance
Lightning Source LLC
Chambersburg PA
CBHW051258250626
47155CB00009B/3346